Tempting Mr. Perfect

Also by Rebecca Rose

Seducing Mr. Right

Tempting Mr. Perfect

REBECCA ROSE

New York Boston

Copyright © 2014 by Rebecca Rose
Excerpt from *Seducing Mr. Right* copyright © 2014 by Rebecca Rose
Cover design by Elizabeth Turner
Cover image from Shutterstock
Cover copyright © 2014 by Hachette Book Group, Inc.

Forever Yours
Hachette Book Group
237 Park Avenue, New York, NY 10017
Hachettebookgroup.com
Twitter.com/foreverromance

First ebook and print on demand edition: September 2014

Forever Yours is an imprint of Grand Central Publishing.
The Forever Yours name and logo are trademarks of Hachette Book Group, Inc.

The publisher is not responsible for websites (or their content) that are not owned by the publisher.

The Hachette Speakers Bureau provides a wide range of authors for speaking events. To find out more, go to www.hachettespeakersbureau.com or call (866) 376-6591.

ISBN 978-1-4555-7791-0 (ebook edition)
ISBN 978-1-4555-8141-2 (print on demand edition)

I'm dedicating this story to my editor Latoya Smith who talks me off the writer's cliff more often than I'd like to admit and for believing in me and my work. Because of you, I'm a stronger writer. Thank you.

To Charlotte Chartier who becomes my muse when mine has deserted me. Our friendship has spanned decades and without you I feel lost. You are my friend, my "sister," my light. Thank you.

Acknowledgments

I need to say a big thank you to my brother Dave for being… well, my brother. You can make the most serious person laugh and would give anything to anyone if it meant brightening their day and therefore, enriching their lives. You have done that for me on so many occasions. I love you.

I'm also giving a big shout out to my fellow author and friend Melanie Meadors who super read this story in one night. You're the best critique partner ever!

To Emma, the sweetest baby girl in the world. You're blessed with wonderful parents and many aunts and uncles. May you always know how loved you are.

Tempting Mr. Perfect

Chapter 1

Kathy Smith walked out of the door without even a good-bye. Dave Sanders's heart sank to his feet while his stomach churned and his mind tried to think of any way to make her stay. Never a man to beg, Dave realized that might be exactly what he would have to do in order for Kathy to open her eyes and see how he felt about her.

Coming around the bar he began closing up the Hungry Lion Bar-n-Grill for the night. Money in the safe, chairs up on the tables, bathrooms empty, all doors locked, lights off. Every night Dave wondered if this routine would get tiring, and to his surprise it never did. He knew where he wanted to be, and every day he came to work was another dream come true—another day that he wasn't using drugs or becoming a statistic for dead drug dealers. Things were perfect for the first time in his life, except for the fact that the woman he wanted walked out after every shift and never went home with him.

The night air hung heavy with the promise that the following day would be stifling. The humidity, thick with dew, left a sheen of sparkling moisture on every surface. Dave swiped his arm across his forehead as he sauntered to the old beat-up truck that he just couldn't part with. The paint had faded, and the body was slightly rusted but the engine purred with awesome power.

Hearing her laugh, Dave turned to see Kathy chatting with the evening waitress, Sue. They were standing next to Kathy's car engrossed in conversation. His heart skipped a beat yet his mind split with opposing opinions. One said to walk over there, grab the chick, and kiss her. The other pushed for him to jump in his car and escape as fast as he could, ensuring his dignity. The meddlesome, internal argument came to a halt when Kathy spotted him. He'd been standing there like a fool, keys dangling from his fingers, staring at the two women. Sue waved him over with a smile.

God, I'm such a dingbat, Dave scolded himself then dragged his feet to join them.

"Dave," Sue said. "You work too much. We were talkin' about going out tomorrow night for a male strip review. Wanna come and perform for us?" she teased.

"Umm...not really my thing, Sue. But you could always try my brother. Jake seems to like taking his clothes off. Remember Sophie finding him in only boxers on the Lion's office couch, Kathy?" He winked at her and from under the streetlight he saw color rush to her cheeks. *Gosh, she's so cute.*

"I might just do that," Sue answered. "You think Sophie would mind? She is his woman now, after all."

Kathy gave a sweet little laugh. "To see Jake naked? No, I don't think Sophie would mind."

Dave shifted on his feet, awkward and wondering what else he should say. Kathy wrung her hands while Sue kept smiling at them both.

"You know, kiddos, I'm gonna run. The husband is waiting and the curtain climbers will be up in six hours."

Dave nodded. "Okay, Sue. See you later."

"Bye, Sue." Kathy waved.

Together they watched her leave, the last lifeline to easy conversation between the two of them. They stood in the parking lot and stared at each other as if their very next words would determine if the sky would cave in and death would be imminent. Nervous tension prickled the air. Hypersensitive hormones made his body aware that a beautiful woman stood in front of him and mating was imminent. Yet something else besides hormones pulled at Dave. An urgency to have her in his arms, a yearning to be so close their bodies and minds would merge into one and drown in the abyss of pleasure, fulfillment, and understanding for what the other needed. His rapidly beating heart clenched from anxiety, as the roaring in his ears submerged the world around them to silence. The thick, suffocating air compressed his lungs, while one single thought repeated in his mind: *Just friggin' kiss her!* They were so close their bodies brushed and she didn't back up or try to avoid his touch when he reached out to her.

"You should go," he told her while his eyes held hers. "It's late."

"You're right."

But she didn't move. No, actually, she quirked her lips in the slightest way, casting a bewitching spell of lust over him. Dave could neither move nor think. A voice echoed in his head: *Kiss me, Dave. Do it now!* With the world around them diminished, Dave brought his lips to hers. Testing, tasting, and cautious. This one kiss was a risk and would open a new chapter in his life. She was the woman he had been waiting to meet for years. Her laugh, smile, understanding eyes, and quick humor were things he longed to see and hear.

Dave's eyes closed, heightening his other senses and increasing his anticipation. With hands gentle and soft, Kathy cupped both Dave's checks then glided her fingers into his hair. Oh, he felt about to come undone. This fantasy, now a reality, was scarcely leaving room for turning back to sanity's door. His mind told him to loosen the stronghold he had around Kathy's body but she felt so right in his arms. And as the kiss went deeper, Dave found his body pressed between hers and her Prius. When she hooked one leg on his hip, he accepted the gift she offered by grasping her thigh and lowering himself so their most intimate points met to create a fierce inferno. Touching her wasn't enough; he wanted more. He needed more.

Tearing his mouth from hers, Dave couldn't deny what was happening between them. "Come home with me," he practically begged.

Kathy opened her mouth and replied in serious honesty, "*Beep...beep...beep...beep.*"

"Oh, what the hell!" Rolling over in bed, Dave slapped the alarm. "Every time I get the balls to make a move on her, I'm interrupted! Damn it!" He threw the alarm across the room where it slammed against the wall, and fell broken to the floor. Hard and sex-deprived, Dave covered his eyes with his arm. "You're pathetic. A pathetic man with a crush." *She's a gorgeous woman who hardly notices you're alive and seems to avoid you as much as she can.*

Showered and testy, Dave headed out into the frosty air. The ground, frozen and slick, welcomed him as he slid into his driver's side mirror. *Great, this has to be the worst winter in New England history!* He rubbed his elbow fast, to help with the pain, then climbed into his truck. *The day will get better, the sun is shining, the birds are chirping, and the truck is fired up.*

Dave kept those happy thoughts in mind as he scrolled through the radio for something to listen to. Turning right on Main, he made his daily stop at the local convenience store. Another coffee for him, one for Kathy, a paper, and Ring Dings—the breakfast for future Olympians. The clerk greeted him with gossip and obituary news, then gave a "See you tomorrow, Dave" before moving on to the next customer.

Back on the frozen road, the old truck gave a lurch and then a belch. Dave didn't pay it much mind because with a twenty-degree blast of frigid air, the old vehicle tended to get temperamental and he couldn't blame it. The weather sucked outside and everyone was coming down with the winter blues.

Cautiously Dave slowed to a crawl at the next intersection and waited for the cars in front of him to move. To his left he could see Kathy in her vehicle waiting for the red light to change. Shaking his head Dave pondered the shy red-haired woman. She was so well put together, mentally as well as physically. He had seen nothing rattle her over the past five months she had worked for him as the Lion's manager. Everything he asked of her, she did. Every blindsided problem, they solved together. Kathy was reliable, smart, and a good person. Dave stepped on his accelerator to catch up with the cars in front of him. His vehicle coughed but began to move through the four-way intersection. His thoughts wandered back to Kathy as he watched the vehicle in front of him pull out of a fishtail. Yesterday she had laughed at his lamest joke, the one about a hippo and the lion. Any woman who laughed at that understood his humor and could capture his heart. Kathy had everything he looked for in a woman and yet she never seemed to have as much interest in him as he did in her. *She wouldn't even share an appetizer with me.* It pained him to think he didn't have what she was looking for in a man.

Dave's truck did a slow slide toward the side of the road. While compensating for the skid he wondered what she would think about his sordid past. Would she be compassionate or do as so many others had? Act as if it didn't matter and then gradually withdraw from him. Heck, maybe she already knew and that's why she never returned his small advances. And maybe—

The crash came first—metal bending, cracking, splitting. Then the jolt—Dave's body twisting, snapping, tearing. With a solid whack, Dave's head hit the driver's side window. For a moment his mind felt stunned from the piercing pain.

Then everything went black.

* * *

As if waking from a dream, Dave's mind told him to move because it felt uncomfortable. However, as he began to shift, he found a restraint across his chest holding him in place. As his body hung toward the right, Dave suddenly realized he wasn't in bed like his psyche had been tricking him into thinking. In reality he was in his now mangled truck that was turned over on its passenger side.

"Dave! Dave! Oh my God!"

The familiar voice penetrated the haze in his mind and forced his eyes to open. A kaleidoscope of color blurred his vision, then the hues slowly melted together to form objects his mind tried to grasp. "Kathy?"

"Yes. I'm right here."

He turned his head to look up, and through the driver's side door he saw her. "Jesus. Am I dreaming?"

"I'd say it's a nightmare." She reached down and touched his check. "The ambulance is on its way."

"Never a nightmare if you're in it." His head became too heavy to hold up. "I think I'm gonna vomit." And he did. The sound of sirens in the distance only made it worse as he reached for the belt that pinned him in place. "I need a napkin and to get the hell out of here."

"No." That one forceful word stopped him.

"Kathy, I'm hanging in my truck and I just upchucked on myself."

"Dave, you may have serious injuries from the jerk who ran the light, maybe even a concussion. Please, don't."

"Agh." Dave brought a bloody hand to his aching head.

"You rolled a spin and a half. The paramedic will help you out, just hang there a little longer." She gave a small chuckle. "No pun intended."

"Are you trying to get a laugh out of me when I was only trying to get your attention?" Dave closed his eyes.

"Well you got it, Dave," she told him in that sweet voice.

He could hear the emergency men asking Kathy to step back, then more glass breaking and a man talking.

"Hey, buddy. How's it hanging?" he asked Dave.

"Not very comfortably right now," Dave told him with a smirk. "You wanna watch your step. I lost my stomach in here."

"I've seen worse." The man supported Dave's neck with a brace before assisting Dave's body with his own. When the seat belt was opened, the man slowly lowered Dave from his elevated position in the truck cab. "What's your name?"

"Dave."

"That pretty lady out there your woman?" As his rescuer talked, he and another man pulled Dave out of the battered truck.

"Future girlfriend if I have it my way," Dave replied.

"Well, I don't think that's a problem now." An icy stethoscope moved around Dave's chest. "Hurt anywhere?"

"My back."

"Move your toes…good. Fingers…good. Now look at the light…follow it…good. Okay, Dave, you're gonna be taking a trip to the hospital. There's room service and nurses—"

"I'm fine." At the sound of a female huff beside him, Dave opened his eyes. "Hi, babe."

"Don't 'babe' me. You have to go. You could be seriously injured. You could have—"

She looked as if she would break into tears at any moment so he reached a hand out to her. "Okay, I'm gonna go. But really, I'm fine. It's just a bump on the head and…and…a—"

Blackness.

* * *

Kathy's body began to tremble the moment she saw the car heading for Dave's truck. Her heart lurched forward in her chest as the inevitable happened. Terror streaked through her as she watched his truck roll over and over then come to rest against a tree. Jerking her car off the road, she slammed on her brakes then sprinted toward the wreckage—and Dave.

"Please don't be dead. Please be okay." Kathy repeated the chant again and again, in hopes the words would make it true.

With one strong jump Kathy leaped atop the overturned truck and looked down through the driver's side window. His body had just been hanging there. No movement, no sounds. She reached out to touch him as her mind reeled with the memories of the man who dangled quietly in the chaos around them.

On her first day of work, Dave brought her flowers. Feeling

enchanted by him and the blossoms, she had kissed his cheek—
a daring move for a woman who preferred solitude. Growing
up with parents as eccentric as hers made being the center of
someone's attention an uncomfortable and foreign place to be.
She had never been anyone's sole focus before and started finding herself slowly pulling away from the man who seemed to be
trying to woo her. The man who made her heart flutter every
time he said her name; the one who evoked in her a curiosity to
know more about him and pulled at her heart to be with him.
Every day Dave was considerate with little gestures like coffee
and bagels in the morning. And once again Kathy had started to
feel the slippery slide of yearning for a husband and a home. But
after her one big mistake—no, mistake wasn't the right word—
catastrophe. Disaster. Humiliation. How could she trust herself
to make an astute decision when she hadn't been able to see Todd
for who he really was? Abuser, cheater, pedophile.

As far as Kathy could tell, Dave didn't have a malevolent bone
in his body. He was as trustworthy and straight-arrow as a man
could be. Immediately a sense of sadness draped its heavy arms
around her. Kathy had pretty much blown him off yesterday after
he had made her laugh with some silly joke then asked if she'd
like to share some food. On a huff, she looked to the hospital's
waiting room ceiling for divine understanding but only received
the intercom calling to a doctor.

*I'm so stupid! Now he could be dead and I missed my chance at
telling him that I care, that I would take a chance at being more
than friends.* Agitated, Kathy let her head fall in her hands. Of
course *now* she was ready to make that leap, and not a minute
before. No, Dave had to be put in harm's way before she would
take that risk.

"Kathy! What the hell happened?" Jake, Dave's younger

brother and business partner for the Hungry Lion Bar-n-Grill, stormed into the waiting room. "Where is he?"

She stood slowly and gave her best friend Sophie—Jake's girlfriend who was also a ballet instructor—a hug. "It was awful!" Tears she'd held back spilled down her face. "I saw the guy coming. Dave pulled out in front of me at the light and…" Her throat burned as she tried to relate the nightmare. As their faces changed from shock to concern, Kathy's heart shredded to pieces from worry.

Stomping away and back again, Jake asked, "What about the asshole who hit him?"

Kathy shook her head. "I don't know. He seemed really drunk. When he climbed out of his smashed car, he stumbled over to Dave's truck and started yelling at him, me, and the EMTs."

"Jerk," Sophie said.

Kathy could feel her breath quickening as her heart raced with panic; her soft, quiet voice rose a pitch higher. "There was so much blood on that jerk's face and he didn't even know it. How could a person not know they're bleeding like that? I mean…it was everywhere."

"Sit down, Kathy." Sophie took her by the shoulders and directed her to sit. "Have the doctors come in and told you anything?"

"They're observing him right now. He definitely has a concussion and maybe a broken arm."

"I'll be back."

Kathy and Sophie watched Jake bolt out of the room. Never known for being a calm man, they could hear him demanding the receptionist get him information on Dave. With a little giggle, Sophie turned back to Kathy.

"Isn't he the best?"

"He's probably intimidating the heck out of that poor woman."

"Naw. He's all bark." Sophie eyed Kathy, as if searching for something she hadn't yet told her.

"What?"

"Are you okay? I know if I saw something like that happen to Jake, I'd freak out."

"I'm all right. Just shaken, is all." *That's an understatement.* Kathy looked down at her unsteady hands. She hadn't been this scared, this upset, since the night she left her ex-husband. His temper was something to be feared, and when he found Kathy packing…she wasn't going to think about it. The past is where it should be and that's where she was going to keep it.

Jolting from the soft touch on her shoulder, Kathy went from examining her hands to looking helplessly into her friend's concerned eyes. "Yeah?"

"You sure?" Sophie asked.

"Yeah. It's just that he's such a nice guy—"

"And you're not used to that," Sophie interjected.

"He brings me coffee every morning." A small smile lifted one corner of Kathy's lips. "He's really sweet."

"He likes you Kathy." Covering one of Kathy's hands with her own, Sophie said, "Dave's not Todd."

"No, he's not." Exhaustion forced Kathy's eyes closed as she tried to block out not just the world happening around her but also the one that never seemed to allow her to move on. "I hope he's okay, Soph. He's a good guy."

"Me too, Kathy. Me too."

They sat quietly for what seemed like forever. People rushed in, people rushed out. Every time a doctor would poke his or her head in, every waiting body would jolt to attention. The purgatory became nerve-racking—to get so hopeful and then find the physician was there for someone else.

Jake finally returned to the waiting room. "Bad concussion. Whiplash, sprained arm, dislocated shoulder and lucky to have been wearing his seat belt," Jake informed them.

Both women let out a long breath.

"He's staying the night and we'll be able to see him in a few." Jake's lips twisted in disgust. "In hospital time I think that means about an hour."

"Probably," Sophie said.

Two hours later Dave appeared doped up on pain meds. His heavy, black-ringed eyes, pale coloring, and slurred speech made it impossible to think otherwise. The heart monitor beside his hospital bed beeped with a consistent lulling rhythm.

"Hey, guys," he said with a lopsided grin.

"Hey, yourself." Jake sat on the bed next to his brother. "You scared the hell out of Kathy."

He turned his cocoa eyes on her. "Sorry. Wasss only trying to get your attention."

She laughed a little at his impaired speech. "You're slurring, Dave."

"Done worrrse."

Jake snapped his fingers in Dave's face. "Yes, you have. How many fingers?"

"Leave him alone, Jake." Sophie laid a kiss on Dave's forehead. "You're a lucky man."

"I know." Dave gave a little smile and moved his eyes back on Kathy. "Thanks."

"For what?"

"Being there."

Kathy swallowed the lump that attempted to choke her. "You scared me."

"And me…myself."

"Okay, everyone out." Dave's nurse announced. "Time for the patient to get poked. You can come back later."

"Tomorrow," Dave told them. "I'm taking the day offff."

Unable to resist the temptation to touch him, Kathy brushed some of his wild hair away from his face. "No problem. But I'm docking your pay."

"I'll tell the boss."

Why did her heart always beat just a little faster whenever he teased her? "Well, good luck with that. I hear he's not gonna be available for a few."

As Kathy walked out of the room with Sophie and Jake, her stomach churned and the sensation to curl him up in her arms then cry thankful tears he was alive almost overcame her. She wanted to stay with him no matter what the nurse said. The emotional pull was as unfamiliar to her as her parents' hippie lifestyle—something she would never understand. When she was married to Todd, she wouldn't have given a second thought about leaving him in the hands of another. Yet concern over Dave's well-being consumed her with the need to stay.

"Kathy? Are you sure you're okay?"

"What? Why?"

Sophie stopped walking and examined her friend. "Because you don't look so good."

"Gee, thanks." Her short defensive answer brought an apology right away. "I'm sorry, Sophie. I guess I'm still a little upset. I really just want to go home and climb back in bed but I have to get to the Lion."

"If you're sure. You know Sue is more than capable of handling things there."

Uneasy confusion brought Kathy's hand to her head to ease the spinning. "I know."

"I'm here if you need to talk. Anytime is never too late or early. I know you care about Dave, and this was—"

"I'm fine, Sophie. Really I am. And Dave and I are just friends. That's it. Nothing more."

"Whatever you say, Kathy."

Kathy's breath whooshed out of her lips. "It's already been a long morning and—" Sophie's surveying eyes caused Kathy to pause. "I'm sorry I don't mean to be snippy. I'll talk to you later. Okay?"

"Okay. But you have to promise you'll call me if you need me."

She hugged her longtime friend. "I promise I'm good, Sophie."

But she really wasn't. Her stomach wouldn't stop turning and her mind's eye kept reenacting the moment of impact. She had a hard time concentrating on the road, that is, once she was finally able to get her car unlocked and the engine started. It wasn't long before Kathy gave up and pulled over to the side of the road just as tears of relief overcame her. She cared for Dave. Kathy realized the enormity of admitting it to herself and the fact that she had been trying to stop it from happening right from the moment they met.

Finding a rough napkin in her glove compartment, Kathy wiped at her tears and the mascara running down her face. *Damaged, used goods.* That's what she was and Dave deserved much better than that. He was a good man who gave back to everyone he cared about. Not like her who had only caused heartache and uncertainty in her own life and others'. *Oh, why can't I be one of those strong women who go after what they want instead of cowering away? Why can't I just say, "Damn it all!" and..."* And what? What would she do?

"I'd kiss him," she told the empty car knowing her secret would be safe. "I'd kiss him and make love to him," she repeated after a long defeated sigh.

Chapter 2

Dave shifted position in his office chair at the Hungry Lion. The sling wasn't just uncomfortable, it was downright irritating—which matched his mood. Twice he tried to take it off, and both times Kathy's inner radar sounded and he got scolded. *Really? All I want is to be left alone.* But Jake insisted on Dave staying with him and Sophie for the duration of his recovery and everyone at the bar kept insisting he should be home healing instead of at work. A perturbed snort escaped Dave's nose. Sophie wouldn't let him be. The first night home from the hospital she woke him every two hours "because of the concussion" when all he wanted to do was sleep. In the weeks following his release, she also drove him to all his doctor's appointments and checked on him constantly *and* without warning. He wanted to scream; however that would only bring more unwanted attention.

Dave shifted the sling again and as if on cue, Kathy sauntered in. "Time for pain meds," she announced with cheer.

"I'm not in pain." Despite his words emphasizing the fact he was tired of being coddled, Dave's mood lightened from her mere presence. "I like you playing private nurse with me and all but when will you stop shoving these pills down my throat?"

Kathy fluttered her long, thick lashes. "As soon as you don't need them anymore."

Dave gazed in her uncertain eyes and realized she was the only person he truly didn't mind being pampered by. It meant that Kathy would be close to him and he could joke and tease her at will. She always lifted his spirits, even when she wasn't meaning to. Hurting her feelings was the last thing he would ever want to do but...an agitated breath escaped his lips. "I understand you're all trying to help but I'm not an invalid."

"I never suggested you were, did I?"

She looked crestfallen so Dave backpedaled to make it right. "No, no. That's not what I meant. It's just forcing me to take pain medicine that I don't think I need. And everyone forcing me to go 'home' when all I want to do is get my mind off the accident by working. I don't want to go 'home,'" he signaled with air quotes, "a.k.a. my brother's house. I don't want to sleep anymore," he grumbled with what he hoped was a very pitiful look on his face.

"Well..." Kathy huffed with a small lift to the sides of her mouth. "So much for me playing the nice nurse. Guess I'm going to have to change tactics." She leaned forward, trapping Dave in his chair by putting a hand on each armrest. "Take the damn pills or I'll call Jake in."

"HA! I'm not scared of him." *She's teasing me* Dave realized to his surprise. And her face was so close to his, another wonder with how aloof she had been toward him only a few weeks prior. The fruity bath wash she used every morning was still lingering on her skin and playing with his libido. Those full, luscious lips that beckoned him every time he looked at her were merely inches away and lightly painted pink. *God, all I have to do is lean in a little more and they'll be mine.* Dave's eyes flicked from her slightly parted lips to her ever seducing eyes. An abyss of concern showed in them along with the potent attraction swirling between them.

"Fine, then I'll call your parents," she told him, breathless.

"Now, Kathy. That's not very nice," he purred. "Gosh, you're the sweetest-sounding woman I've ever met, Kathy Mae."

"That's what all the boys say," she flirted, triggering immediate color to creep into her cheeks. Then her cell phone chimed, breaking the playful banter. After making an agitated grunt she hit a button and the jingle silenced.

Oh, he liked it when she got feisty. It turned him into mush and made that night's dream of her so much more erotic. "I bet under all that sweetness there's a wild woman waiting to be released."

"First of all who says I've never let her out?" she asked while caging him back in on the chair. "And, second this isn't about me. It's about you taking your medicine."

"I'm fine, Kathy," he told her while leaning in closer. "You, on the other hand, look as if you're needing a massage."

"Mmm. That may be but—"

He couldn't count the times he wanted to touch her in those soft denim jeans that her legs were currently filling out so well. Gliding his good hand up her thigh, over her hip, to rest on her tiny waist, Dave could honestly say he just crossed something off his bucket list.

"Dave," she said in a winded voice, "this is—" She pulled back and sat on the edge of his desk. A weak smile formed on her lips while her eyes filled with unshed tears.

"I'm sorry, did I do something wrong? I thought we were… you know, connecting." He pulled a hand through his hair. Kathy said nothing, only looked down at her hands while a line of worry crossed her brows. "Kathy?"

"I thought you were going to die, Dave. When that car slammed into your truck I...was so scared," she whispered. When a tear rolled down her sharp cheekbone, he stood and wiped it away with his thumb.

"No, no. Don't do that. Please, Kathy. I'll take the pills. I'll go home. I'll sleep." Nothing had him fall to his knees faster than a woman weeping. And right now he'd give her anything to make it stop.

"I'm sorry. It's just that I'm trying to help take care of you but you seem so miserable most of the time and I don't know what to do."

"I know and I appreciate it. But I need my own bed. Kathy, *please* help me. My brother and Sophie are driving me nuts and I'm going to lose it on them."

"Sophie likes to take care of people."

"So do you." He gave her red locks a tussle with his good hand. *Soft as silk.*

"Thank you."

Dave covered her hand with his and in a leap of courage leaned forward and kissed her lips.

Kathy jumped back and stood quickly. "Dave, you need to take your pills. Here." She placed them on the desk next to his coffee. "I'll see what I can do about Jake and Sophie." With that said she bolted out the door and left him wondering if maybe he should have let her make the first move and if he had just destroyed his only shot at being with her.

* * *

With intense concentration Kathy stared at the Lion's office wall as she talked to Sophie on the phone. "Did you know Dave serves the homeless every Thanksgiving? Isn't that so sweet? And a couple years ago he and Jake sent their parents to the Caribbean on a cruise."

"I heard their mother drank too much and ended up on the captain's lap." Sophie laughed.

"I can't even imagine liking my parents enough to send them on a cruise. Of course that wouldn't stop them from trying to get me to pay for one."

"That sucks, Kathy. Have you heard from them?"

Kathy twirled the phone cord around her finger. "No. Hey, did you see the story on those elderly people who were scammed by that couple down in Connecticut? They took those poor folks for twenty thousand."

"I saw that! Not to mention the break-in down the street from me yesterday. It got Jake so worried he put extra locks on our doors."

"Dave offered to have Jake come over and do the same for me but I don't want him to get the wrong idea. Like I can't take care of myself or something."

"I doubt he'll get that out of extra door locks, Kathy." On the other end of the phone Sophie took a long breath. "I don't understand. I thought you liked Dave."

Their kiss bloomed in her mind awakening her body with subtle warmth. She had truly wanted that intimate touch, longed for it, but couldn't risk leading him into thinking they might have some kind of future together. "I do, I did, but now…I don't know."

Longtime childhood friends, Kathy could always rely on Sophie to get right to the point. "What aren't you telling me, Kathy?"

Sophie's tone was as irritated as Kathy felt but what could she do? She grew up with neglectful, free-spirited parents who thought

nothing of swapping sexual partners, giving their children marijuana contact highs, and letting their only daughter get involved
with a man who took her tender innocence, leaving her leery of
trusting anyone—including herself. All her life she avoided getting too intimate with men because even her father had never been
a source of trustworthiness. Sophie, on the other hand, may not
have had the most supportive parents but they were there when
she needed them—they were there when Kathy needed them, too,
when at the age of fourteen she tried running away.

"Dave kissed me this afternoon," Kathy confessed.

"What? When! I want all the details."

Kathy brooded. "You're not supposed to be excited. You're
supposed to see how confused I am."

"What's to be confused over?" Sophie asked. "He kissed you."

"Believing he doesn't only want sex from me is so important.
I don't want casual sex. I want trust, heart-wrenching passion, a
connection soul mates feel."

"How did he kiss you?"

"I don't know. He just kissed me." What did that have to do
with anything? A kiss is a kiss, right?

"Was it slow and sweet? Fast and passionate? What led up to
it? Come on, Kathy, don't make me drag this out of you."

One hand holding the phone, Kathy covered her face with the
other. "He did take a bad bump to the head. Maybe he didn't
know what he was doing. Just forget it. I'm having a lousy day,
that's all." Kathy started to wonder if maybe she had been the
one who got a good clonk on the head. Dave was her charming
boss, nothing more, and yet…every time he brought her coffee
with a smile and a wink, she melted a bit more. The way his shirt-
sleeves hugged those muscular arms and broad chest always made
her body tingle. And his voice—tough, rugged, deep.

"Kathy?"

"Yeah?"

"What else happened? I know you too well. When you begin a conversation like this and then start thinking a way out of it, something's really bothering you."

"Is that what I'm trying to do? Shoot." Kathy picked at her favorite sweater. "I'm trying to get out of that habit."

"And have been doing a pretty damn good job. Kathy, don't let past baggage get in the way of happiness."

"I'm not, Soph." With a cleansing breath, Kathy confessed to what she hadn't realized was actually bothering her. "He told the EMT that I'm his future girlfriend."

"Whoo. Umm, well…how do you feel about that?"

Never one to jump into anything without thinking it through first, Kathy spoke carefully. "He's seeing something that isn't going to happen. Or he's hoping for it. I'm terrible at relationships. Heck, I ran when he kissed me and that was only a peck. There's seriously something wrong with me. " Kathy argued with herself. "I'm dysfunctional when it comes to connecting with people and opening up to anyone besides you. You know what? Forget it. I'm doomed to a life alone. I should get twenty cats, learn to knit, and let my hair grow in gray."

"There's nothing wrong with you. You're a beautiful woman who's had a tough life. He's a good guy. Trust me, I wouldn't lie to you."

"I know you wouldn't. Maybe him being *too* good is the problem. What if it's more of the mind-numbing relationships I've had in the past? I want a normal relationship with an ordinary guy but I don't want it to be so 'safe' he becomes boring. I also don't want a criminal who brings cops, lying, and cheating right along with him. Is that too much to ask for?"

Sophie's hesitation to answer was loud and deafening to Kathy's troubled mind. "Is there something you want to tell me, Sophie?"

"Nope."

"I've worked with Dave for five months and all I've seen is the straightest most generous man on the planet. Heck, he swore in front of me the other day and apologized." Kathy picked up her cold coffee and drank. Despite everything she said, the image of Dave's sexy body bending over in front of her and his tight buns beckoning to be squeezed materialized in her mind. But maybe she shouldn't mention that to Sophie.

Sophie's laughter rang through the phone. "I think you might need to get to know him a little better. Yes, he a good guy but he's—"

"He's like the best big brother in the world. Look what he's done for Jake! Dave's kind-hearted and I don't want to break that."

"Kathy, trust me when I say Dave feels he's paying a debt to Jake and their parents. Besides what the hell are you looking for? Another man to treat you like shit?"

"No!" Kathy startled at the knock at her office door. "Hold on a minute, Sophie. Yup?"

At the sight of Dave in the doorway her body refused to move while her brain began to scramble for something to say other than, "Ahhh...Hi."

"I'm going home. To my home. Can you give me a ride?"

Did he just ask me something? She had seen his lips move but hadn't heard a thing he said. No, her eyes were too busy looking at his good arm where the sleeve was rolled up. The boa constrictor winding its way from his elbow to his wrist demanded her attention. Mixing that with his disheveled hair he looked absolutely rugged and downright delicious. When the scent of his cologne snaked its way to her senses, Kathy's toes curled and her leg muscles tightened. *Aggg, this would be so much easier if he didn't always look and smell so good.* She couldn't quite pin down the right way to describe his scent but it always reminded her of rebels and wild nights.

"Umm, yeah. Just a minute…or two…I think." *Jesus, he must think I'm a total nutcase!*

"Great. Thanks." Dave hesitated briefly then closed the door.

"I'm bringing Dave home. Damn that man confuses me. I don't want to be attracted to him. Do you hear me, Sophie? I shouldn't be ogling him and yet here I am talking to him like I left my brain at home this morning when he only asked a simple favor of me. I've always been able to talk myself out of being in love, like, and anything in between when it comes to a guy. Why is it not working with Dave? Well?" Kathy could hear the misery in her own voice.

"Because you should give him a chance and open yourself up to the possibility of real love."

Kathy let a long exhale go before she replied. "I need time and he needs you and Jake to lay off of him. Apparently you're driving him nuts."

"I saw it coming this morning when he growled at me. Even Schnitzel is sick of him."

"Schnitzel is the fattest cat on the planet and has an attitude anyway." A small chuckle escaped Kathy as a smile turned up the corners of her mouth.

"I rolled over in bed yesterday and my foot touched him. The cat had the audacity to hiss at me. Jake says it's gonna take time for him to get used to me. I say if the cat keeps it up, he's finding a new place to sleep."

"Your first lovers' quarrel. How sweet."

Sophie scoffed over the phone. "Our first. Yeah, right. Okay, you have a man waiting for you. And, Kathy?"

"Yeah?"

"Give Dave a chance. He might surprise you. That's all I'm gonna say."

"What's that supposed to mean?"

"You'll find out."

"Sophie, this isn't fair. You can't leave the conversation after saying something like that."

"I will." Then she hung up.

"Damn you," Kathy ridiculed.

Being in the car alone with Dave was going to be tough because she couldn't figure out how she was going to convince them both that there was nothing happening between them if he started cracking jokes and melting her heart. After grabbing her jacket and purse, she walked into the bar area dragging her feet. The Lion wasn't hopping but it wasn't deserted like a few weeks earlier when a deep freeze had shut most businesses down for the day. New England spring had finally broken through the icy shell of the last storm and raised the temperature to a nice sixty-three degrees. The winter cleanup had now begun with large lumbering trucks fixing pothole-ridden streets while other work vehicles were trimming trees and grinding their fallen friends. The winter had been a long, snowy, cold one and the relief of it being over was evident in the way people were smiling. *Well, most people. Dave sure doesn't look happy at the moment.*

"Well, if you think of anything, Mr. Sanders, it would be appreciated. Not that I expect much from you."

Kathy glanced at the police officer talking to Dave, then to the two Hungry Lion regulars, Louie and Stuart. They were leaning forward on the bar watching with obvious interest the interaction happening before them.

"Sorry, detective. I can't help you." Dave appeared more than defensive. He looked downright obstinate, from the way he stood with his legs braced apart, to the arrogant tilt of his head. Kathy found it intriguing to see that her good-guy boss had a temper.

She shot the two men at the bar a warning look, then asked, "Can I help with something?"

"This doesn't concern you." Dave's response brought a raised brow from Kathy.

"Well—"

"It doesn't matter anyway. The officer was just leaving. Weren't you?"

Not knowing what to say, Kathy remained quiet as the officer nodded to them both. "I'll be in touch."

"I'm sure you will and the answer will still be the same. I can't help you."

Anger rolled off him while his body stood rigid and the arm resting in the sling had fingers fisted tight. She placed a hand on his shoulder and Dave shrugged it away.

"Can you just take me home?"

"Fine," she told him with a scowl.

They walked to her car in silence. *What could the cop have said to put him in this bad of a mood?* "Did it have to do with the accident? Is the guy getting off?" she asked curtly.

"No. Nothing to do with that." Dave kept his eyes focused straight ahead on the road.

"Okay…well what did it have to do with?" When Dave opened his mouth, Kathy sneered, "Oh yeah, it 'doesn't concern' me."

Dave remained silent.

"Well, you don't have to be a jerk about it." *So much for being a nice guy.*

Kathy shifted uncomfortably in her seat while Dave continued to seethe. The silence coexisted between nerve-racking and pleasant. *I don't want to talk to him anyway,* she told herself. That was until they arrived at his home and another cop stood there waiting.

"Really? What the heck, Bennett?" Dave yelled as he got out of Kathy's car and marched toward him.

"I told that detective you weren't gonna have anything for him," Bennett said.

"Well, I don't." Dave unlocked the door then turned to Kathy. "Thanks for the ride."

"Is everything okay?"

"Fine, thanks. You can go."

"And miss this?" she snickered. "I don't think so," she said, in hopes of breaking the tension and staying with him a little longer.

Dave visually ground his teeth. "I don't want you here."

Despite all the self-pep talks Kathy said, "I don't care. I'm concerned."

"Bennett, please tell the lady she needs to leave before you remove her from my property."

Kathy turned a wicked glare at the officer.

The officer looked at Dave then back at Kathy. "Ma'am, I think you should go."

Dave didn't turn to look at her, only opened his front door and went inside. "Come on, Bennett."

Fury swelled up so fast, so potent, Kathy thought she would spit nails at the both of them. He was just like all the others before him who said they cared and then treated her like crap.

Well she wasn't going to take being walked over anymore. "You son of a bitch!" She raged while stomping into his house.

"Look, Kathy, this isn't the time. You've made it clear that you don't want anything more than friendship with me—that distance is what you want. Now I'm giving it to you and you're pissed."

"I care, Dave, and don't deserve to be treated the way you're treating me right now."

Dave visibly took a deep breath. "When I came into your office you hardly talked to me. You acted as if I was just bothering you. Sorry if I inconvenienced you, Kathy, it wasn't my intention."

Oh, he hadn't "inconvenienced" her at all. He had totally surprised her into silence with that tattoo that made her mouth water. But she wasn't going to tell him that. "And what was your intention?" she finally asked.

"You know what? It doesn't matter now because I see how wrong I was."

His hurtful words and insolence caused Kathy to rethink the forwardness of her actions. Was she doing this because she wanted to know what was going on or because she had actually started to care for him? She could only stare at Dave, her mind blank, waiting for someone to write on its canvas so she would know what to say next. His sudden anger was frightfully tantalizing and sent a quiver of desire rushing through her body. Dave wasn't the dull, normal type of man she usually dated. There wouldn't be any "Let's sit and talk about this." Or "We should meditate so we don't turn our energy dark." No, Dave seemed to be equally as sour as he was sweet, and it would have been a refreshing change if insecurity wasn't roping her back into the box she had fought for years to get out of.

As he popped a beer, Dave looked at Bennett. "This is my new manager slash accountant at the Lion, Kathy Smith. Kathy this is Officer Bennett. Bennett and I have been friends for a really long time. If you need any paperwork, Bennett, my books at the Lion are clean—"

"That won't be necessary."

Dave fixed his eyes on Kathy. "Bennett and I have some things to go over. Thanks again for the ride."

Kathy trumped down her inexplicable disappointment. "Nice to meet you, Officer Bennett."

"I'll see you around, Miss—"

"Kathy," she told him while ringing her hands. "Goodnight, Dave." She turned and dashed out the door and to her car. Choking back tears, Kathy wondered what she was thinking.

"Kathy?" Dave's hesitant voice came from behind her just as she reached the car door. "I'm sorry. You didn't deserve to be treated that way."

She kept her eyes focused on the ground because the last thing she wanted to do was look at him and begin crying. "I don't know what I was doing. I had no right to be forceful with you."

His hand cupped her chin and raised it so their eyes met. "I don't want you involved in this."

She nodded her head as her heart skipped and her body became keenly aware of how close he was.

"I liked seeing you getting all aggressive with me, Kathy. You've got more spunk than you let on. Very, very sexy," he whispered and brought his face closer to hers.

She pressed her lips together to prevent a smile from fully forming. When the tingle deep inside her body rose up to heat her neck and settle on her cheeks, she knew she was done for. "Well damn, Dave. What am I supposed to say to that?"

It showed in his eyes—the intent before the action. Her mind told her to move, avoid the kiss by putting a restraining hand to his chest, yet her heart allowed her to do nothing. And just a fraction before their lips touched she closed her eyes, tipped her face up in invitation. Yes, she had been dodging his advances but something had changed. Now she wanted Dave to make her feel what no other man ever had. As his lips caressed Kathy's, a deep craving to be touched shook her soul and propelled her heart into conflict with her mind. Her hands shot into his hair as his body pressed her against the car.

"I don't want a relationship, Dave," she said against his impatient lips.

"Then maybe you should stop kissing me." His challenging eyes stared into hers. "Go ahead, try to stop."

Her brain told her to push him and his arrogant dare away while her hand fisted the front of his shirt and brought his tempting mouth back to hers. What was she doing? This wasn't part of the "stay away from Dave" plan.

"I thought you didn't want this?" he asked before shifting his mouth and fastening it on her neck.

"I don't."

"Then maybe we should stop," he said with a smirk.

Kathy could feel the heat of the humiliation on her cheeks for him to see. "What? Oh my God, you're a jerk. You did that because you knew you could and I'd...I'd—"

Dave rocked back on his heels with a smile on his face. "Enjoy it? Want to kiss me, too? What's so wrong with that?"

"Everything!" Kathy jumped into her car and peeled out of his driveway. Getting away from him was the smartest thing she could do for herself. Dave had just proven that he could take advantage of her and she'd go willingly.

"Stupid! Stupid! Stupid!" she yelled at herself even as the

thought of him taking advantage of her body and them laughing in bed afterward became a very real and welcoming vision.

* * *

"Still making a good impression on the ladies, I see," Bennett announced as Dave walked into his kitchen.

"She says she's not interested in me." Dave could see Bennett trying to hold back a chuckle.

"That's not what I saw."

"Yeah, well, you're an old man who needs glasses."

"And you're a guy who trouble likes to find, even when you're on the right side of the law."

Dave rolled his friend's words over carefully as Bennett sat down at Dave's kitchen table. Why did his past always have to sneak back up and remind him of the man he used to be? He should just stay away from Kathy and save them both from wasting their time.

Bennett looked around the kitchen and shook his head. "I didn't think you'd be able to change your life around, Dave. No offense but there's very few people in this world who have the kind of strength and determination it takes."

"None taken." Dave sat across from him, beer in hand. "What the hell is going on?"

"Trouble. It ain't got nothing to do with you. They're only followin' every lead—old and new. There's been a series of break-ins lately and you'll most likely see Detective Owen again. He's in charge but don't worry; as long as you've been on the up and up there's nothing to worry about."

"I can't get any more normal, Bennett." Dave studied his drink before taking a sip. "Strange that after all this time I still feel like running when I see you at my steps."

Bennett laughed loud. "Just as strange as me still thinking you're gonna."

It was an hour later, while walking Bennett to his car that Dave thought about how he had run for too long and for all the wrong reasons. Even as Dave watched Bennett drive away, appreciation overcame him. That man had busted the rowdy kid Dave had once been too many times to count. Bennett told him that if he didn't straighten his act out he would end up in jail—that happened—or he was going to die—that happened—or he could be "the lucky son of a bitch who turned his life around"—that happened, too. But there was still a void in Dave's life that he couldn't shake.

And suddenly his thoughts had returned to Kathy. She brightened his world whenever she came around. He found himself searching her out at work to ask silly questions, just to hear her voice, see her smile, hear her laugh. He felt complete when around her. As if nothing in the world mattered except her, him, and what could be. What he felt for her pushed him to do things he would never have done to or for any other woman. And the spell she cast upon him only seemed to get stronger with every intimate touch they shared.

Dave let out a long, low whistle. That kiss in his driveway had been *hot* and proved to him that despite every excuse she laid out, despite her hesitation toward them being more than friends, she must have felt what he did. He only hoped she still did when she found out about his past.

Chapter 3

Kathy was tired and cranky after the sleepless night spent thinking about what happened with Dave. She looked in the Lion's bathroom mirror and sighed. *Really Kathy. You'd think you could've done a better job with the makeup this morning.* She waved herself off with disgust. Maybe she should see a shrink. Only a crazy woman wouldn't want a man like Dave. He was funny, dependable, loyal, and obviously had a wilder side she hadn't seen yet. The image of his tattoo was one Kathy still couldn't get over, causing her to wonder if there was more to him that she might someday discover.

"Aaggg." She had been so pushy with him yesterday. What the heck had gotten into her? Never in her life had she been that demanding. If someone said to stay out of it, that it wasn't any of her business, she walked away. Why couldn't she do that with Dave? And when he kissed her, her persistence increased to whole new level. *WOW.* The lingering effects were enough to jumble her thoughts of him. Kathy was slowly realizing the more she discovered about Dave, the more she wanted to get to know him, kiss him, touch him, run her fingers over his—"Stop. Stop.

Stop. He's your boss and, and…" She couldn't think of anything else to finish the sentence because the image of them naked, sweaty, and panting popped into her mind. "I'm sunk," she told herself in the mirror.

Kathy exited the ladies' room and walked smack into a patron. Her hands went instantly to the man's broad chest while her feet backed her up against the wall.

"Careful," the man smiled. "You almost ran me over."

His charming smile and face were pleasant enough but Kathy felt no enticement toward the stranger. *Maybe I'm defective.* The thought depressed her as it always did whenever her lack of physical attraction to the opposite sex reared its ugly head—in defense she crossed her arms tight.

"Sorry." She looked down at her feet, not knowing whether to run or flirt with the man.

"No worries. You come here often?"

"Yes…I mean…I work here." *Damn, why do I always have to stutter?*

"Oh?" The man backed up a little and Kathy let out the breath she'd been holding. "I'm Ben." He extended a hand.

"Kathy." Uncrossing her arms she shook his hand. "Sorry."

"It's okay, I'm not fragile. So are you a waitress?" He winked.

"No. I'm…umm…"

"Adorably shy?"

Kathy rolled her eyes. "Why do people always say that? Being an introvert isn't adorable, it's torture." She straightened her shoulders and pushed her quiet voice up an octave. "I'm the manager."

"Neat. I heard the Halloween party last year was a blast. You havin' another one?"

"I think so." Not knowing what else to say, Kathy moved around Ben. "I have to…get back to work."

"See ya around?"

"Yeah, sure."

"Hey Kathy, can I talk to you for a minute?" Dave's voice vibrated through her body. She hadn't even seen his approach.

"I'll be right there, Dave."

"Boyfriend?" Ben asked.

"Boss." With a weak smile she said, "See you around."

My God! How corny can I get? "See you around?" Why can't I ever come up with something sharp and witty? Even as a child Kathy had been the quietest out of every group. Her parents, "the hippies" as she liked to call them, certainly weren't mice. Heck, they'd even gone to Woodstock, the hippie fest of the sixties, with their own parents.

"Yes, Dave?" she asked, while walking into his office. *Don't look at him then he might see how much you've been thinking about him.* Kathy sat in a chair across from his desk and pondered. The man before her was still Dave. Nice, responsible, understanding, dependable Dave. Yet hearing his voice for the first time today, remembering the look in his russet eyes before he kissed her yesterday, proved he affected her more than she wanted to admit.

"About yesterday." He took the chair next to her and turned it so they would have to face each other. "I have to apologize for being such a jerk."

"No need. I was being pushy. I don't know why. I guess curiosity got the best of me." Kathy clasped her hands together on her lap and Dave covered them with his good one.

"Doesn't matter. I was wrong and shouldn't have taken my anger out on you."

"Is it possible for you to get any nicer?" She laughed. "It's okay. I just want to make sure you're taking care of yourself." Kathy bit her lip then moved on. "I'm the one who pushed the issue, Dave. Yes, you were a jerk, a big one, but you did have a good reason."

"That's it? I'm forgiven?" Dave sat back in the chair and smiled.

"Only if you forgive me for being so pushy with you." A painful lump formed in her throat but Kathy pushed on. "I'm sorry about *everything.*"

"Everything?" He winked at her.

She shifted in her seat while her body heated in response to him referring to their kiss. "Umm…yes. I wish you'd take better care of yourself and not worry so much about the people around you."

"I was thinking about you last night."

"Oh. Well, that's nice but you're there for everyone but yourself, Dave," she responded, trying to change the subject. "Who helps you out? Why do you try to push everyone away who wants to help you?"

A crease formed between his brows. "I don't get you, Muffin." Kathy watched and said nothing as Dave stood and began to pace the office. "When we first met, it seemed like you liked me. Then you backed off for what reason, I don't know. Now you seem interested again but when I kissed you, both times, you basically ran away from me. And I'm the one pushing everyone away? It looks to me like you're doing the same thing," Dave froze for a moment to turn and look at her. The passion she saw in his eyes melted all the reserve she had left.

"Dave…I—" She rose from her chair and in a flash was wrapped around him, needy and wild. His lips were a delicious flavor, salty yet sweet, and she wanted more of it. Plunging her tongue in, she invited his to dance. Dave answered her fiery craving by pulling her close. The internal blaze combusted into a million tiny fires and caused every nerve in her body to blaze sensitive and hot.

Dave gently drew back. "Kathy, what the hell was that?"

"I've never felt this before." She confessed against his avid lips. He pulled her closer forgetting about his bad arm and grunted in pain.

"I'm so sorry. I hope I didn't hurt you. It's just…" Her eyes met his. "I have this need to touch you, have you touch me everywhere. It's overwhelming. I don't know what to do anymore because it seems like I'm starting to lose control. Damn it, I was just sitting there, Dave, listening to you, and the next thing I know I'm throwing myself at you." She covered her mouth in shame. "I'm so embarrassed. I've never done anything like this." She felt her face redden at the declaration and Dave's questioning eyebrow.

"You fooled me. I started thinking you weren't interested because you kept blowing me off. But then you do something like this and I don't know what to think."

Kathy stood quietly trying to figure out what to say. Why couldn't she be the smooth talker Sophie always was with men?

Dave took a step closer. "What is it? What turned you on? "

She laughed at him before lowering her eyes and picking at her shirt. "I don't know what just happened but it never has before."

"Interesting." Dave rocked back on his heels.

" 'Interesting?' Are you serious? It's mortifying. I'm telling you that I've never had a man do that to me before, that I've never, never…"

"Never what?"

He'd been so good to her, such a gentleman. Damn Todd for pointing out what a failure at sex she was—how turning a man on and keeping him interested weren't attributes she possessed. Kathy raised her chin and took a deep breath. "I've never been with a man who's given me what I needed."

"As in?"

"Really? You're gonna make me say it? Bastard," she whispered.

"Now that kinda talk is just a turn-on," Dave joked and Kathy attempted a smile.

She couldn't believe how easily Dave stimulated her with just a kiss. She could only imagine the things he could do with her body. The thought drew a wave of lust over her.

"I've never...you know." She motioned with a hand for him to finish the thought.

Dave blinked once, then twice. An astonished realization covered his face and Kathy hid her humiliated one.

"You mean you've never been aggressive with a man? Just taken what you wanted," he asked. "Not even with your ex-husband?"

"My marriage to Todd was a huge mistake, Dave. I was so young when we got together and he was so much older that I thought my lack of sexual knowledge was the problem. After him I dated a few men and still had the same problem." Kathy sank to her seat in palpable shame. It burned hot, acidic, and made her head thump. "The truth is, I'm a miserable failure in the sex department. Defective."

Dave sat next to her and placed a good-natured arm around her shoulder. "Anytime you want to sexually harass me, I'm more than willing to let you. But—"

"Here it comes." Kathy closed her eyes tight. "This is mortifying."

"I'm not the nice guy you think I am. There's a lot you don't know and a promise I'm keeping."

"Like what?" With her interest piqued, Kathy looked at him. "Did you forget to put the toilet seat lid down?"

He laughed hard. "Man, I wish it was that easy." The corners of his serious eyes crinkled while he stroked a finger down her throat to between her breasts then around each of them in a figure eight. "Let me show you you're not defective, Kathy. Your inadequate ex couldn't handle a woman like you. You need a man who will want to please you. Strip your clothes off slowly, and kiss every inch of that incredible body while you beg for more, discover what it takes to drive you wild beyond reason, that's what I want to do for you if you let me."

She knew her mouth had dropped. No man had ever touched her like that or suggested doing such erotic things to her body. Kathy wanted more. She yearned for Dave to do it all, every naughty thing he could think of until her body rejoiced, exploded, and became his. But could he, or was he all talk like every other man she'd been with?

With a possessive hand to the small of her back, Dave leaned into her and began to nibble on her neck. Next he moved to her earlobe where he gave it a gentle tug with his teeth.

"Dave, I really want that but I've always failed the men I've been with and I don't want to do that to you."

"Stop thinking, Kathy. Just feel," he told her while kissing her eyelids.

"Dave, everyone I've ever let in has hurt me and giving into this desire for you...I don't even know what will turn me on. How are you supposed to?" With heat swirling in her most private parts, Kathy closed her legs tight to try and ease the need to be touched.

Dave moved his mouth to her ear. "That's the most exciting part. Learning your body and watching you go over for the first time after you've begged me for relief; being witness to this discovery, as I slide deep inside you."

Dave's words had Kathy burning with desire, a thought that was both scary and thrilling. She turned to him knowing the heat in her face, for once, wasn't from shyness but from passion.

"I want that, Dave." Courage overcame her and brought with it a sense of freedom. Feeling brave, she began to nibble on his chin as her hand snaked its way up his leg toward his crotch. He stopped her inches away from its desired destination.

"What?" she asked in confusion.

"Not yet. You have to work for it," he told her.

Stricken by his bravado, Kathy sat rigid in her chair. "Excuse me?"

Dave winked at her then stood. "I'll see you later."

She couldn't believe he had the audacity to walk out on her. *The nerve of that man!* Storming out to him seemed like the logical thing to do. He'd stirred her up, made her body pulse, and then left. *How dare he?* And to say she'd have to "work for it"? *Challenge accepted,* though not in the way he imagined.

It was at that moment she decided to make *him* beg for *her*.

Chapter 4

Walking through the house toward the kitchen, Dave's thoughts turned to Kathy. He couldn't get the image of the way she bit her bottom lip out of his head. It was a tell sign when she was concentrating on something. He could go on and on when it came to all the adorable things Kathy did and it made him want her more. And then he thought about the kiss they shared.

Dave couldn't help but think about all the ways he was going to have her in bed and decided it would only be his imagination that held him back. And maybe time. He flexed his shoulder in response. And what the hell was up with her ex? How could the man not see what had been right in front of him? She was beautiful, smart, funny, sensitive, and deserved to have a man dote on her every chance he got.

Despite how hard she tried to fight it, he knew she had feelings for him. He could see it in the way she looked at him when she didn't think he noticed. Or the way her body responded to his touch. "But maybe you should stop this whole thing before one of you gets hurt," he grumbled. The fact of the matter was sooner or later she was going to find out about his past and then she'd dump him like every other woman had. And yet he couldn't help how he felt about her.

Grabbing a can of tomato soup, Dave struggled to get it open. "Damn it!" Things just weren't that easy when you only had one arm to work with. After the lid popped, he poured its contents into a pot and turned on the stove.

"Meal for the rich?" Jake's voice boomed through the silence.

"As a matter of fact, it is. What brings you by, besides making fun of my handicap cooking abilities?"

"If you didn't want to live with us anymore, you only had to say so." Jake placed his hand over his heart. "It broke me a little to know you weren't honest with me."

"It wasn't personal."

Jake may have been the little brother but they watched over each other as best friends would. There wasn't anything they wouldn't say or do for one another—and Dave thanked the heavens for that every day.

"Nothing personal? Psss. That's not how it feels."

"Jake, if I tell you the truth you'll just get mad and try to beat me up. I'm not feeling up to it."

"So you want me to wait until the shoulder is better?"

"Well, that's the nice thing to do." Dave's lips cracked into a smile. "But of course, you've never been nice."

"And you've always been ugly. Where's the beer?" Jake plopped himself down in one of the kitchen chairs. "The least you could do is offer me one."

"I don't have any."

"What!"

Dave shrugged his brother's exasperation off. "I forgot to pick some up."

"Bullshit. Come on, Dave, where's the—wait a minute, why are you still smiling?"

Dave couldn't stop grinning, and knew it had nothing to do

with his brother's impromptu visit. "I'm happy to be home and out of yours."

Jake glared at him. "Why out of mine?"

"Because your cat sucks. Schnitzel is the meanest, fattest, most territorial cat I've ever met and I couldn't stand sharing space with his smelly butt anymore."

"He's not smelly," Jake grumbled. "And you were in his space, how would you react?"

"It's a cat. Not a human. See, I told you you'd get upset if I said why I couldn't stay there anymore."

"Because of my cat." Jake seemed to think this over. "Bullshit."

"Fine. You and Sophie were starting to smother me. Not that I don't appreciate what you've done for me but damn, Dude…"

"Oh, you mean Sophie was smothering you? Well, when you see her, you better make sure to tell her you left because of Schnitzel," Jake said with a look of amusement.

"No problem. I'll lock it in the vault for when I need her on my side. 'No really, Sophie, he told me not to tell you.'"

"You do that and I *will* beat your ass. So why are you smiling?"

Dave threw a pot holder on the table then brought his small pot of soup over. "I already told you."

"Eating right out of the pot, eh? Classy man. No wonder Kathy is thinking twice about you. You're a real catch."

With the spoon halfway to his mouth, Dave stopped and studied his brother. "Who says Kathy's thinking twice about me?"

"No one." Sitting back with his arms crossed, Jake grinned at his brother. "Although she did call Sophie right after you left work today."

Dave stirred the soup in front of him and pretended to take this little bit of news lightly. "So. She calls Sophie all the time." He shrugged and ate.

"She was excited."

Now that news got his attention, and before he could cover up his concern, it seeped out of him. "Really? About what?"

"You tell me. When she first came to work for us you were all puppy-dog in love with her. Then...I don't know what the hell happened and now you two are smiling and happy and shit."

"We've decided we're both mutually interested in each other."

"How mature," Jake teased.

"Hold on a minute." Dave walked to his basement door, threw it open, marched down the steps, and grabbed the case of beer he'd been holding out on. "I think we're gonna need this."

Jake took a bottle with a mini-salute. "Sometimes I don't think you want me drinking your stuff."

"Most of the time I don't," he said with a laugh. "Now what was she excited about?"

"Should you be drinking that with pain pills?"

"Stop stalling. And I haven't taken the pills in days. Haven't needed them. Now, spill."

"Okay. I guess Kathy's had some..." Jake scratched under his chin. "Unsuccessful relationships."

"Yeah, she told me." Dave wiggled his brows. "I can help her with that."

"Ummm, not sure I want to know what you're talkin' about but I meant that she gets rid of them before it gets too serious."

"And you think she's gonna get rid of me?" Dave ate his tomato soup and followed it up with a chug of beer.

"I just don't want to see you get your hopes too high and—"

"She got rid of them because they weren't fulfilling her *needs*. If you know what I mean."

At the announcement, Jake spit his beer out like a water sprinkler. "Come on, Dude!" Dave jumped up and began to try to wipe the splatter from his clothes. "You could have led up to that." Grabbing the dish towel, Jake began wiping his mouth and then the table.

"Yeah, you better clean up this mess. Damn, you even got the floor."

"We're off subject. Geez, no wonder she got rid of the ex and those guys. What kind of men has she been dating?"

"None like me." Dave concentrated on the label of his drink. "She hasn't said much about the former husband. Do you know anything?"

"Nope."

Dave could visualize the two of them together walking through the park holding hands, laughing, smiling, and planning their future. *Whoa, slow down buddy!*

"Hey, you took a side trip on me." Jake waved his hand in front of Dave's face. "I said she's never had a reformed trouble-maker before."

" 'Reformed troublemaker,' not sure how I like that."

"It's what you are, big bro, and should be proud. Not too many people can say they lived *and* changed their life."

Dave scratched his head. How much should he tell her? A little? A lot? All? "You know, the weirdest thing happened today. Yesterday Kathy saw me talking to the cops. Before that she pretty much wanted nothing to do with me. Today she's all over me. I mean, attacked me." He gave a slow whistle. "Insane, all…over…me. It was awesome. Hot. If I could have stripped her there, I would have. Unfortunately I got only one arm for the next few weeks."

"Quiet, shy Kathy? Are you sure it wasn't her evil twin?"

"She doesn't have one."

Jake snickered. "Oh man. Sexually repressed women are the best! They'll do anything."

"You're such a pig." Dave picked up another beer and handed it to Jake to open. "Jake, I really want to get to know her. I mean, I think she's it for me."

"Oh man, don't tell me you're seeing white picket fences, children, and tiny dogs."

Dave pressed his lips together to stop himself from saying, "Yes."

"You are!" Jake yelled and stomped his foot for emphasis. "I can't believe it."

"Jake, I want to get to know the side she hides from everyone. Come on, you must have felt that way with Sophie."

"Nope. It was all sex."

Dave gave his brother a bland look. "And I'm sure Sophie feels the same way."

"Nope. She thinks I fell head-over-heels in love with her and will do anything for her."

Dave took a sip of his beer while eyeing Jake. "So you bringing her breakfast in bed on the weekends and giving her foot massages has nothing to do with loving her?"

"Nope. It has to do with the fact that without her I'm lost and I want her to know I appreciate her putting up with my crap." Jake grinned at his brother. "Love has nothing to do with it."

Dave laughed. His brother had just described what love was, and he had a feeling Jake knew it. "So you're saying I shouldn't get to know her."

"Oh, you should. Totally and absolutely. This way you can mush her up with the things she likes and you get to reap the benefits."

"Like sex," Dave stated for clarification.

"YEAH. And don't forget having someone to talk with at night. I mean it was all good and everything when I hung here with you. But having Sophie there all the time is a bonus, and Schnitzel doesn't say much."

"Except when he's hungry."

"Right."

"So sex, talking, massages, breakfast in bed. In that order?"

"Well, not always." Jake shrugged. "But it sounds like a solid plan to get you started. Anything you want me to do? Like get you some candles and sex toys?"

"I don't want your used crap."

Jake kicked back in his chair. "Suit yourself. But don't be going to Sophie for ideas. What we do in bed is our business."

Giving his brother a mild look, Dave said, "Yeah right like I need tips from you and Sophie. You've forgotten who you're talking to."

"Might be time to get out those spare handcuffs you stole off of Officer Bennett."

"I gave those back. And, Jake?"

"Yup."

"If you're going to drink my secret stash of beer, stop insulting me."

"It's all brotherly love."

* * *

Sophie's quick feet gave Kathy vertigo—the dizzying sensation leaving her breathless. *How can a person move that fast with so little effort?* The dancer spun as if gravity didn't exist. Every jump, leap, and promenade convinced Kathy more and more that her friend's talent was actually a supernatural power. How else could a body bend and float beyond all logic?

"Kathy!" Sophie wiped her face with a towel. "I didn't hear you come in."

"I wanted to talk. Sorry if I'm interrupting."

Sophie gently touched Kathy's shoulder. "What's wrong?"

"What isn't wrong? Why can't I be spontaneous, rebellious, sexy—"

"You are sexy. What's this about?"

"Why couldn't I be born with soft curves like my mother? Why did I have to take after my father? Ugh, look at these man hands!" Sophie's long sigh gave Kathy's plight little comfort. Over the years the conversation may have been visited many times but at this moment it seemed more urgent than ever.

"You are beautiful. Now what's the matter?"

The negative energy of Kathy's thoughts sucked every ounce of self-worth from her. She had begun to question her life's path and the results were painful. "I'm not sure if this is right. If things don't work out with Dave, I'll be out of a job and it took so long to find one after I was laid off."

"Dave wouldn't fire you, Kathy. Come on over here and sit down." Sophie led her friend to a nearby couch. The soft, pale shade of pink accented the ballet studio nicely.

"I remember picking this out," Kathy said while rubbing the plush material.

"It was fun."

They sat there in silence for a few moments. "I'm not sure if what I'm feeling is the product of a self-made pity party or a well-deserved crisis."

"Either one is good. What's going on with Dave?"

Kathy's eyes rolled to look at the ceiling. "The man is driving me nuts. I don't understand. It's crazy. I'm crazy. He's so darn adorable with the way he taps his pen against his desk when he's trying to figure something out. Then there are those biceps of his that seem to constantly be flexing. I want to grab him, throw him to the ground, tear off his clothes and…well, that's just it, I'm too afraid to take what I want." Unable to stay still, Kathy rose to her feet and walked to the ballet barre. "How can you get your leg up here without pulling all your muscles?"

"Years and years of practice. What do you see in Dave's eyes?"

Turning to look at her friend, Kathy leaned back against the wooden handrail. "You're gonna think I'm nuts."

"Already do."

"True. Okay, I don't know if I'm ready for a man like him."

Puzzled, Sophie asked, "I don't get it, what do you mean?"

"Whatever's between us is overwhelming. I feel like if I allow this thing that's happening, I'll lose all control and…Sophie, Dave looks at me as if he wants to eat me." Kathy winced. "That didn't come out right."

Sophie laughed goodheartedly. "Yes! Kathy, my friend, you are going to learn what it's like to have a man take care of all your needs. You're feeling desire, lust, attraction!" She jumped up from the couch and danced a little jig. "I can't wait."

"Geez. You'd think you're the one who might get laid."

"Oh, I get that every night, and twice on Sunday," she added. "But you're going to have your first orgasm. I can see it!"

"You're creepin' me out," Kathy sobered.

"Kathy, you owe it to yourself and him to give this a real chance. Otherwise you'll always be asking yourself 'What if?' and that'll stink."

"You're right. I know you're right. He's the first guy I've ever felt this kind of attraction for and it's not just his chest under those tight shirts, or his arms, or his butt. It's how I feel when I'm with him. He makes me laugh and feel sexy. When he looks at me, I mean truly looks at me, I swear he can see my soul because he always knows the right things to say and do. Aagggg."

"We need to go shopping!" Sophie announced. "Get you some new spring and summer clothes. Have ice cream and talk about our men."

"Dave isn't my man." Not yet anyway. But did she want him to be?

"Oh, Kathy." Sophie put a reassuring arm around her friend's shoulders. "I'm telling you this time will be different. Don't think on it too much."

"Yeah, yeah, I know. Don't try too hard. Let yourself relax. Be patient, it will come—no pun intended. The right man just hasn't met you yet."

"Yes, he has. Come upstairs. I want to shower before we go shopping."

"I don't want to go shopping," Kathy miserably mumbled.

"Yes, you do. Now stop feeling sorry for yourself and come with me. You're going to relax and tell me everything that's happened between you two while I get ready."

Chapter 5

With the end of the week here and a successful shopping trip done with Sophie, Kathy headed to the grocery store. She was thankful to see the crowd wasn't as overwhelming as she feared with Easter coming the following day.

A display stand in front of the chips and cereal aisle called her over. What could she do but give in? After all just because her family never celebrated it didn't mean she couldn't take advantage of all the yummy chocolate that came out during that time of year. Yesterday at the end of the work day, Dave had given her chocolate-covered strawberries in a heart-shaped box. The note attached simply said "You're beautiful." She gushed over the card for hours and then put it away in an old wooden keepsake box she kept in her nightstand drawer. No man had ever been so sweet.

Kathy picked up a chocolate bunny and noticed the label wasn't to her specifications. If she was going to cheat on her diet then she was going to *cheat* on her diet. From behind her a dark chocolate bunny with a caramel middle hopped into her line of sight. The hand holding it bounced the tasty treat.

"You want me me! Don't go for that generic junk, you're too classy," Dave told her in a mock bunny voice.

Laughing, Kathy took the Godiva bunny. "You're absolutely right. I'm a Godiva girl." She turned to Dave with her lips pressed together in an attempt to suppress her amusement. "How about you?"

"Guess," he said with a wiggle of his brows.

His eyes twinkled with mischief and Kathy accepted his invitation to play. That something special about him pulled at her and the closest she could come to putting a name to it was comfort. She felt that, and peace—he gave the world around him a solid foundation for all to stand on. But what intrigued her most was what she didn't know about him. *How odd that he can be both soothing and mysterious.*

"I'm gonna guess jelly beans and Peeps."

He leaned in and gave her a peck on the lips. "You know me well."

The quick kiss left her wanting more and wishing she was brave enough to kiss him back while in public. "I bet you were the kid who put the sweet yellow chicks in the microwave to see them grow."

"Nope," he corrected her. "I liked seeing them explode."

"You would!"

They stood there for a moment staring at one another; silence preluding more to come.

"Kathy, would you have lunch with me?"

While her mind stumbled, her heart was confident. "Yes. But aren't you at the Lion today?"

"I called Sue in to cover for me. Figured I deserved a two-day weekend."

Kathy looked at her basket of groceries and Dave's cart. "That's a lot of food for one person."

"Jake and Sophie are coming over tomorrow for Easter dinner and my parents will be up sometime next week. Why don't you join us tomorrow? We'll be eating at two."

With one hand up in protest, Kathy declined. "I don't want to intrude—"

"You won't." He took her hand, brought it to his lips, then smiled. "Have lunch with me today. Give me a chance to change your mind about joining us."

"Are you a romantic or just out to seduce me?"

"A little of both."

"Okay. Lunch."

"Great. Let's pay and get out of here."

"But I'm not done." Panic streaked across her mind as she glanced at her basket.

"You don't want to buy anything perishable anyway. It'll go bad in the car."

"But—"

"Actually maybe we should just leave our stuff." Dave looked as if he was seriously contemplating the idea.

"You can't do that!"

A little wild-eyed, Dave told her, "But I don't want you to change your mind."

"I...no...I mean. I won't. Promise."

The look on his face was the picture of Christmas morning and Kathy had to smile.

"You won't run?" he asked in all seriousness.

"No." How could she? His presence alone had brightened her day.

"Okay, let's go." He dropped the chocolate bunny that started it all in his cart then nodded his head for them to go to the cashier.

"So where do you want to go?" The sun glistened off his brown hair and Kathy glimpsed the blond highlights that were sure to become lighter in summer.

"What do you like?" she asked.

"Italian, American, Chinese, sushi, you name it, I'm all over it." His body bobbed in excitement.

"I love sushi." She giggled, while realizing the full scope of Dave's boyish cuteness. How come she had never noticed it before?

"Awesome. I know this great place. Let's take my car and we'll come back for yours."

"Umm, okay."

He grabbed her grocery basket and tossed it into his cart. "Come on. We'll beat the lunch crowd."

"Dave, slow down." Kathy lengthened her stride to catch up with him.

"Sorry."

The big-toothed grin he gave her on top of the disheveled hair that currently stuck out everywhere on his head made Kathy laugh harder than she had in months—possibly years.

"You laughin' at me, Miss Smith?"

"Yes." She covered her mouth to stop the snort that was sure to come next. "I just never realized how truly adorable you are."

"Oh, I'm cute. And sexy," he replied, and pulled her into his arms. "You though...you're stunning."

She let out a huff. "Really, Dave? You're so going to give me a big ego."

"It's okay. I can handle that." Staring into her eyes, Dave brought his mouth down to hers. Unhurried and ever patient she understood the immense need inside him when he grasped her behind and crushed them together.

"Jesus, Dave. You're walking around like that?"

He stayed close to her, letting their breath mingle. "This is what you do to me, Kathy."

Dave was hard. More than that—rock solid. And she blushed from the intimate knowledge. "We should probably check out and get to the car."

"Right. The backseat is better for what I'd like to do to you, though."

"No. no." Horror hit her fast. What if Dave took her right there in the parking lot and she was a letdown for him like all the men before him?

"Kathy, calm down. I'm only kidding. Here, help the invalid put the groceries on the belt."

She stood there grinning; trapped between delight that they ran into each other and wonderment that she never knew this fun side of her existed. "Maybe I don't want to," she teased.

"Really? Hmm, how about another kiss of persuasion?"

"Oh, you're very good at coaxing people, aren't you?"

"One of the best." He cupped the back of her head with his hand and pulled her in for a slow, gentle kiss. "Now help me with the groceries."

"Okay, Mr. Sanders. But I'm not going home with you to unpack them," she said while helping empty the cart.

"And here I was hoping you'd come over and do some cooking and cleaning."

"In your dreams!"

He paid the cashier and they walked out to his car together. "Lunch awaits, my lady," he said after opening the passenger side door and sweeping a hand out in invitation for her to sit.

"I think this is our first official date, Dave." Kathy's insides danced with excitement as he kissed her lips once more.

"It's been a long time since I've been on one," he told her. "Please be gentle with me."

She sat in his car while taking notice that the world around them seemed to be sparkling. Was it because spring had finally come? Or was it because of the man who sat next to her?

"I was thinking," he told her, "maybe we can neck after this. Just to make sure I still know what I'm doing."

"Somehow," she answered as her heart swelled inside her chest, "I don't think that's gonna be a problem."

* * *

Kathy reeled from her date with Dave. She couldn't hide her excitement.

"And then we went to a movie and ate a crap load of popcorn. After that he brought me back to get my car and we said good-bye. Nothing to it. Easy stuff. I don't know why I still feel so nervous. I mean, geez, the movie had this really hot sex scene and I could feel my body turning really, really hot and when I turned to Dave, he—oh it was so romantic—he took my face in his hands and kissed me." A long breath escaped Kathy's lips. "I have to say, I was a little disappointed that he didn't even try to make a move on me. But then I realized we *were* in the movie theater. And then—"

"Kathy?" Sophie's soft voice sounded sleepy. "I'm really tired. Can we pick this up tomorrow?"

"It's only eight. Are you feeling okay?" Sophie never got sick. She always had enough energy for five people to live off of. But her voice sounded weak and Kathy felt a little guilty for not realizing this earlier.

"I'm fine. Think I've been burning the damn candle at both ends for too long, that's all."

Kathy's lips moved into a pout. "Jake should be taking better care of his woman."

"Yeah."

Again her feeble voice alarmed Kathy. "If this goes on for more than a few days, you should go to the doctor."

"I have an appointment Monday morning. I'm just run-down. How about we catch up when I see you tomorrow?"

"That sounds like a plan."

"Okay, I'll see you at Dave's for Easter dinner."

Excited about her date and Easter dinner the following day, Kathy couldn't hide her excitement as she walked into her kitchen. Suddenly her cell began to ring. The caller ID displayed a number she didn't recognize so she shrugged and ignored it. But after it stopped ringing, her landline rang with the same unfamiliar number.

"Hello."

"Hi, Kathy," the quiet voice said.

She froze for a brief moment before saying, "Stop calling me, Todd." She hung up as the revolting flavor of disgust filled her palate. When her landline rang again Kathy simply picked up her keys and left both her apartment and her cell behind. She needed to buy a dessert for tomorrow anyway, and the Italian bakery around the corner boasted about having the best baked goods in town. Hopefully by the time she walked back Todd would have gotten the clear message of "Leave me alone!" and stop calling her every damn week.

It was the aroma in the shop that hit her first and tickled her nose. Everything smelled sweet, and her mouth watered as she looked over the bakery display case in front of her.

"Hello, Karma, I mean Kathy."

Kathy turned to the voice behind her and came face to face

with her ex-husband and father's best friend—Todd. He was much older than she remembered and his thick mane of hair had grayed and thinned. Without thinking she took a step back as ice froze her veins. Fear came first then defiance toward this unwanted confrontation with a man she never wanted to see again.

"Your parents told me you moved into this area." He flashed his charming smile, the one that once made the teenage girl in her giggle but now made the grown woman's skin crawl.

"They seem to have big mouths." To not waste any more time on him, she turned and walked out of the shop door. Damn her parents! They must have given him both her number and address.

"Kathy. Please wait. I didn't mean to—" When he took her arm with a solid grip Kathy swung a flat-palmed hand hard against his face.

"Don't touch me," she hissed.

Onlookers stopped to stare as Todd rubbed his check. "I can't believe you did that. Apparently I still need to remind you of your place. You haven't grown up very much."

"Apparently I have. Do you still get a thrill out of knocking women around and taking advantage of young girls?"

"Kathy, you weren't young, you knew what you were doing. You *wanted* me to teach you; practically begged me to." His eyes were almost black from the contempt he obviously held for her.

"I was too young, by the standards of the law and in the mind. You're disgusting." Looking him up and down Kathy couldn't remember why she'd once found him attractive. Of course any sixteen-year-old who had the attention of an older man who insisted on how pretty she was, wanted to take her away so they could live free on a beach and watch the sun set every night, would fall for the lie. He "understood" her and how she didn't fit in with her family. She was different…special, and that's why he loved her. Loved her? Is that why when she was eighteen she found him in bed with her parents only months after she and Todd were secretly married? Kathy's stomach clenched from the memory.

"I lov—"

"Don't you dare say it. Your warped sense of love isn't real. It's perverse."

Todd narrowed his eyes. "Kathy, you've changed."

"A lot has happened in ten years." She started walking away in hopes he wouldn't follow but his steps behind her said otherwise.

"I want to talk to you. Clear the air." He tried to grab her arm again and Kathy yanked it out of his grasp.

"Go to hell. That's where your type belongs." Kathy made it just past the building when she stopped and turned on him. As she stood there her body quaked, snapping the restraints that had held her down for too long.

"Sweetie, I'm dying."

She scoffed and would have been horrified with herself if this conversation had involved any other person. But this was Todd—a family friend; her father's best friend; her ex-husband; her parents' lover and the man who took her innocence in a deceptive way.

"Dying?" She could feel the shameless satisfaction on her face.

"I can't believe you can be so cold-hearted to smile." Tears sprang to his eyes, one even escaped down his cheek.

She leaned her face close to his. With a black heart full of malice, she said, "I hope whatever is killing you does it slowly and without mercy." Her words came naturally as hatred ripened in her. "You deserve no forgiveness because you've never felt shame over what you did."

Todd stepped back from her, disbelief apparent on his face. "I...how could you?"

"How can I? How could you think that coming here and finding me was a good idea? Did you think I would fall into your arms and weep?" Kathy wanted to do more than just punish him with her words, she wanted to destroy him. Have him feel what she felt, or lack thereof, for years now. This man had stunted and ruined her for having any form of a healthy relationship with a man. "You were already dead to me when I found you with my mom and dad."

Todd rounded his shoulders back and lifted his chin. Kathy remembered that response whenever his word was questioned. "That was a misunderstanding that *you* blew out of proportion. I told you the truth and you didn't want to listen."

She sneered. "Yes, finding you all in bed naked was a misunderstanding. Not to mention the fact that my mother, herself, tried to compare sex stories about you with me! Sick. That's what they are and that's what you are."

"But you forgave them." His eyes were of a man who'd been beaten down to nothing. Yet the show of remorse didn't soften her. Instead it made her stronger because she knew what a snake he was.

"You're very misinformed," she told him.

"You can't forgive me?"

"Forgiveness is for the one who's giving it, not receiving it." Kathy looked around them and saw a few people standing around watching the confrontation. Even the man from behind the counter of the Italian bakery had come out. He nodded to her and she acknowledged him back.

"I need yours," Todd pleaded.

"You came to the wrong person. I'm at peace with my parents.

They are who they are and I can't change the fact they're my family. You on the other hand, I can cut you out and never have to think of you again."

"What happened to you?" Todd swallowed hard and shook his head with a tsk-tsk.

"I grew up and discovered that my father's best friend was a pedophile and my parents covered it up. How many states is it now that you can't be in?" Kathy advanced on him quickly but halted when they came toe to toe. "You make me sick."

Todd placed a trembling hand on his chest. "I'm so sorry for what I did to you."

"No, you're not. It was all a show then, like it is now." Kathy took a good look at him. She started with his tattered shoes and moved up to his worn jeans that boasted many holes. His stained shirt looked to be more than a decade old and his skin's sheen was yellowed with malnutrition. Todd looked like a homeless man. She sniffed and realized he probably hadn't showered in a while, either.

"I forgave myself, Todd. For ever being naïve about you and me. You lived life how you wanted."

"I had a right to and you're no one to tell me that was wrong."

She saw the intent in his eyes; Todd had always been a very physical man when provoked. She felt a ping of pleasure knowing he could never hurt her again.

Bringing her mouth close to his ear, she whispered, "Go ahead and push me. Hit me. I know you want to. But remember I'm not a teenager anymore. Dying or not, I'll kick your ass."

Where had she found this strength? Never in her life had she stood up and said, "Go to hell" to anyone. Even when she left her parents' way of life she did it without much of a fight. Kathy simply packed her stuff, wrote a note, and moved. No fuss, no arguments. They hadn't been happy but the one positive quality about her parents was they always wanted whatever their two children wanted. Well, that and they preferred it being just Evaan and Telia. Many times they would talk about how much fun they had and all they did *before* having kids. Kathy never wondered why she had attachment issues.

"I came to say good-bye, Kathy."

"Don't bullshit me. You came to see if I'd show you mercy. And from the looks of you, you probably hoped I'd let you stay with me." His eyes darted to hers. "Forget it."

With that Kathy walked away. She never looked back or had a split second of guilt over how she left him. No, the only thing she felt was freedom and the churning in her stomach.

She almost didn't make the bathroom before she purged herself. Violent tears and gut-wrenching sobs came at once. When she was done, relief filled the empty space.

Hope sprang inside her. Maybe she wouldn't be so defective now. Perhaps seeing Todd was exactly what she needed to finally move on with her life.

Chapter 6

"Hey, Jake?" Dave looked over the bar and at his brother. "You hear about the convenience store robbery the other night?"

Jake passed a patron a drink. "Yeah, that poor cashier is lucky to be alive. Hear she took two bullets."

"I'm thinking maybe we should update the security system."

"I'm thinkin' you might be right."

"You still doing that cancer walk with me?" Dave threw the bar towel over his hurt shoulder then adjusted his sling. "One more week and this damn thing can come off. I can't wait." *And then I can get both hands on Kathy.* He couldn't wait for that either. The last couple of days had been torture. Stolen kisses here, caressing each other there. She had showed up early for Easter dinner and because Jake and Sophie hadn't arrived yet, Dave pulled her into the house, pushed her up against the wall, and kissed her until he felt both their knees go weak. Her tentative hands had explored his body and if Dave concentrated hard enough, he could still feel them roaming under his shirt. He couldn't be sure what was driving him crazier, the lack of use of his arm, or the throbbing in his groin.

"Arm bothering you?" Jake swung around the bar to help with some of the tending duties since the Friday night crowds were starting to get a little louder and more demanding with the warmer weather.

"Naw, this contraption really isn't comfortable, that's all. So the cancer walk, you coming?"

"Not yet. But hope to be doin' that tonight with Sophie." Jake wiggled his brows and then passed a woman a drink.

"You can come with me, big boy," the woman said to Jake.

The comment earned a whoop from Louie, who was also helping out behind the bar until Dave's arm was better. "You got a live one there, Jakie!"

Ignoring his coworker Jake leaned on the bar and gave the woman his best smile. "You're lovely but I'd be putting your life in danger."

"And how is that?" She stroked a single red nail down the front of his chest.

"My lady would kill you. You see I'm her slave." He winked and then backed away.

"He's telling the truth. Can't get him to do anything without her okaying it!"

"Louie, shut up," Dave advised without any real force.

"She's very lucky. If you change your mind, I'm right over there." The woman pointed to the back pool table room.

"Hate to break your heart, honey, but I won't be changing my mind."

"All the same. You know where I am." She sashayed away and Jake licked his lips while Dave rolled his eyes.

"Dog."

"Nope. Just real lucky. Sophie plans on running the five miles. I told her she'd be on her own with that 'cause my knee's been acting up."

Dave snickered. "I only run if someone's chasing me."

"Then you're outta shape, bro. Been a while."

"You're telling me!" Actually it'd been about ten years, after Jake had committed himself to the military but before he'd been shot. Relief washed over Dave as he looked at his brother. Jake had been in a dark place when he returned from war and was never hesitant to tell people he only survived because his friends and family battled to save him. Dave frowned because he couldn't say the same loyalty happened to him. No, when he was lying comatose in the hospital, his "friends" had stolen from him. But then again that's how he found his way back to the people who meant the most, so how could he regret it?

"Is Doc Murphy going to make it?" Dave asked with caution. Doc was a fellow comrade that Jake had met at group therapy. The man had really been lost but in the last month there'd been some kind of change. He was over at Jake's house when Dave first met him, and while the man said little, you could see so much mayhem in his eyes. Dave had seen that look before in Jake's and was glad that Doc had someone to lean on.

"No, but he said he's gonna work toward doing it next year." Jake swigged some water. "He went to see his kids on Easter."

"Wow. Good for him."

"He's doing all right." Jake smiled.

"Where is the little lady tonight?" Dave asked to lighten the mood.

"Sophie or Kathy?"

Dave's lips twitched, "Both."

"Right." Jake took his time answering, knowing the suspense of the question would be agony on his brother.

"Jake?"

"Yeah?"

"I think the table over there is getting a little out of hand. Wanna talk to them?"

They both looked toward the far wall. Four guys were playing darts, getting snookered, and harassing the waitress. "Love to. Oh, and they're shopping again. I don't know how many clothes one woman needs. But I told Sophie that she's going to have to stop because there isn't enough space in the house."

When Jake straightened and pushed his shoulders back, Dave grunted.

"What?"

"Jake, you're going to scare the hell out of them. Try not to look so intimidating. And put your arms straight down at your sides."

"I can't and you know it. Too much muscle." He smiled.

"And not enough brains?" Dave gave him a good-hearted punch on the shoulder. "Only kidding."

"Ha. Ha."

With the sound of the bell chiming over the door and the sight of Kathy gliding in, Dave's world came to a screeching halt. Her eyes were different. She'd done something wicked with her makeup to make them appear larger and they watched him as he did her.

"Hi," she mouthed.

He nodded to her just as one of the troublemakers stepped in his line of sight, so close to Kathy he could see the guy's body rub against hers. Every muscle in Dave's body tensed and he immediately filled with a need to protect her. He took off his sling at the same time the man put a hand on Kathy's arm. Dave didn't know where Jake went, and he really didn't care. Kathy was his to take care of and no one else's. In the weeks they'd been getting to know each other, Dave could tell something ugly had happened to her. It was the reason she was so careful and timid around him.

Coming around the bar Dave saw every move the man made, and Kathy's protests. She jerked her elbow out of the stranger's hand when he tried to get her to go with him. And when Sophie tried to interject, the aggressor put his back to her and kept his attention on Kathy.

"Come on, baby, I can show you such a good time."

"I don't need or want your kind of a 'good time.'" Though painfully shy Dave saw Kathy's hand fist and didn't doubt she would use it if she had to.

Dave's thirst for blood overcame any rational thought and when the man reached for Kathy again, Dave spun him around and socked a fist to his nose. Blood spattered everywhere and the women gasped as he laid down one more powerful blow that knocked the man to the floor unconscious. Arms large and wide wrapped around his chest and pulled him back. He didn't even give a hint of struggle to his restrainer—his opponent was down.

"Jesus, Dave."

"You were too slow, what was I supposed to do?" When Jake released him, Dave walked over to Kathy. "Are you okay?"

Her wide-eyed stare gave Dave a moment of worry. *Shit, what if I scared her?* Instead of being angry with him, Dave found himself encased in her arms. She dove at him with vital urgency. Never in his craziest desires had he imagined she might take him in front of an audience. And while the idea excited him, he worried she might not be okay. Slowly he moved her to arm's length. "You're okay?"

"I'm so sorry." She looked bewildered and ready to run. "I can't…I…you saved me."

"You need to sit down." Sophie guided her to a chair.

"Thank you so much, Dave," Kathy said, wrapping her arms around herself.

Dave watched with amusement. "Wow. I can't say I've ever had this type of effect on a woman before."

"Hey, buddy!" A drunken man said from behind Dave. "What the hell was that about? I called the cops. I'm having you arrested."

"Perfect. It'll save us from kicking you guys out for harassing my staff." Dave turned back to Kathy who continued to stare at her feet. "Kathy do you want a wat—?"

"I'm talkin' to you, man!"

Dave felt the heavy hand lie on his shoulder but it never got a grip. Jake picked the man up and tossed him across the room.

"You touch my brother again, and I'll mop the floor with your face. We understand each other?" The other two men with the perpetrators nodded then knelt down to examine their friend who still lay out cold. "Louie! Call the cops again."

"Sophie, you okay?" Kathy asked her friend.

"I'm fine, just a little thirsty. You want water? I'm getting one for myself."

"Yeah, thanks."

The whine of sirens felt more like a relief than a nuisance. Dave cleared his throat. "Listen up, everyone. Whatever you ordered tonight is on the house," he announced.

"What?" Louie and Jake turned and glared at Dave.

Lifting his hands to gain attention, Dave spoke loud and clear to his listening customers. "I'm sorry if this spoiled your evening, folks, and I hope you'll come visit us again."

The door chime sounded and four cops, including Detective Owen, walked in. Dave bit back an oath.

"Check that man!" Owen ordered and one officer jumped to get it done. "Trouble, Sanders?" He pointed his question to Dave but Jake answered.

"Yup. Four guys who couldn't handle their beers. This sad-looking one on the floor assaulted our manager."

"I see." Owen's eyes never left Dave's. "How's the arm? Thought it was still in a sling."

"Yeah, well the sling got in the way of me defending my own."

* * *

The exchange between Dave and Owen was painful to watch. The only thing the standoff was missing was a western dirt road, six-gauge shooters, and dusty hats. Heck, Kathy could've been the damsel in distress. The thought seemed deplorable except for the fact that Dave would be the one riding to her rescue. The image of him in chaps, spurs, and a cowboy hat made Kathy's thighs tighten. She searched the crowd of people for a rescue from her erotic fantasy. Sophie had gone to find some rags for the bleeding men and Jake was giving information to one of the cops while keeping a hawk's eye on his brother.

"Ma'am? Are you all right?"

"Hmm? Oh, yes. I'm fine." Owen and Dave eyed her as if there was another head about to sprout off her neck.

"Can you answer some questions?" Owen's eyes were soft, and he didn't seem like such a bad guy even though Dave clearly thought so.

"Yes. I'm not sure what I can tell you. I had only just walked in."

"From what Mr. Sanders says, the guy manhandled you, thus causing the commotion. Ex-boyfriend?"

"That's not what I said," Dave seethed.

Maybe she was wrong. Maybe this cop was a jerk. "I don't know what you're talking about. I've never met those men before. From what I can see, I don't believe they're regulars and if you're suggesting that by walking into my place of work I started this, you're wrong. These men obviously can't hold their alcohol." Dave gave her a sly grin at her response.

"I wasn't suggesting anything, Miss…"

"Smith."

He wrote it down on his little note pad. "Smith. Is that your real name?" Owen's eyes bore into hers while waiting for an answer.

"Detective," Dave interrupted, "can Kathy give her statement tomorrow?"

"Yes, I would really prefer that," she told him.

When the detective smiled at her, Kathy's skin began to crawl. The man was more than a little overweight, balding, and ridiculously sweaty despite the cool temperature in the bar. The sensation of being naked and vulnerable seemed to go hand in hand when he set those beady eyes on her.

"She seems perfectly fine to me," Owen said.

"That's because you don't know her."

When Dave put a protective arm over her shoulders, Kathy couldn't stop herself from leaning into him. Warm, safe, dependable. He was all those things and so much more.

"I'll give you my statement then, too." Dave told Owen. "Jake!" he yelled before the officer could protest. "I'm driving Kathy home. Mind?"

The giant of a man walked to them then pulled Kathy into his arms for a hug. "You okay?" More than a little shocked at his openness of affection, Kathy only shook her head. "Get some sleep and take tomorrow off."

"I'm fine and more worried about Sophie. She's really not feeling well." When the men seemed to be examining her, she asked. "What?"

Dave ran a hand over her thick, red hair. "You're shaking that's how I know you're not okay."

"Really?" She looked down at her trembling hands. "Oh, guess I am."

"Let me get my sling and talk to the staff." As if in reflex, Dave shifted his shoulder and adjusted his back with a grunt.

"You hurt yourself."

"Naw. Only a tweak."

"You've experienced worse. Right, Mr. Sanders?" Kathy, Dave, and Jake all looked at Detective Owen.

Jake crossed his massive arms. "Detective, I just have one question. Why are you here?"

"The call came in and I responded."

"But this isn't your normal thing, is it?" Jake stepped closer to Owen, who held his ground.

"No."

"I'm gonna be completely honest with you, detective. I think you only came because you knew this was our place, specifically, my brother's."

Owen clearly mulled this around in his sweat-beaded head. "What are you accusing me of, Sanders?"

"Gunnery Sergeant Sanders if we're going to do this properly. I think you heard something went down at the Lion and you wanted in on it because you think Dave's—"

"That's enough Jake." Dave abruptly interrupted his brother.

A look of disgust crossed Jake's face but he backed down. "I'll be in touch, Detective Owen."

"Nice bodyguard," Owen mumbled while Jake walked away.

"I don't need one. Card?" Owen pulled a business card from his front pocket and handed it over. "We'll talk tomorrow," Dave told him.

"Good. I have lots of questions. Miss Smith, were you injured at all?"

It was too obvious Owen was stalling them. Kathy knew the moves. How many times had her parents been detained for one reason or another? Most times with threats that their children would be taken away if they didn't conform to what society deemed acceptable. Or about them not holding down steady jobs and scoffing about being suspected drug dealers. The clincher always came when they would openly admit to being swingers and that hanging out with known pedophiles wasn't against the law. Yes, Owen only wanted to see if he could bring Dave's temper back out. Well she wasn't going to give him that chance. "I'm fine, thank you. Can we go now, Dave?"

"Yeah, let's go."

"One more question, Miss Smith."

She turned a wicked look on Owen. "*Yes,* detective?"

"Do you feel safe working here? I mean after tonight, of course."

"Jackass." The word slipped out and when she looked at Dave both his brows were perked to attention. "Let's go."

She could hear her heels clicking on the wood floor and feel the furious beat of her heart pounding in her chest. *The nerve of that man! Thinking he could get her to second guess working for Dave! "Is that really your name?"* The detective's sarcasm echoed in her mind.

Kathy swung the bar door open as an older couple came upon it. She stepped back and held the door for them. *No sense in being rude and spreading the bad karma around.* Kathy laughed at herself because her brother loved teasing her with that line.

"Oh my! What's happening here?" The older woman, who seemed to be as tall as she was wide, asked.

"I don't know, my love, but I hope it's nothing serious," the tall gentleman answered.

Kathy smiled. "I can assure you it's only a few boys getting rowdy."

The woman put a hand to her ample breasts. "Thank goodness. Look, there's Jake." She cupped her hands around her mouth and…"Jake! Over here! Jake!"

"Mom! Dad!" he called back. "Dave, Sophie! Look who's here!"

A smile bloomed across Dave's face. The love for his parents was apparent as he ran to hug and kiss them. "What are you doing here? I thought you weren't in until tomorrow."

"Well Jake called the ship, when you didn't," his father said while giving Dave the stink eye, "and we got here as soon as we could."

"Dad, you and mom have been saving for that month long Hawaiian cruise forever, don't tell me you cut it short."

"No, no. He assured us you were okay and that there would be hell to pay if we did. But we did change our flight to tonight instead. And we're staying for two weeks instead of one," their father explained.

Gosh, Dave looks so adorable standing there. Kathy took a step back to let the family hug and say hello. She only made it two steps before Dave took her arm.

"This is Kathy. Kathy, my father, George, and my mother, Renee."

"Is this 'The Kathy'?" Renee inquired.

"Yes," Sophie piped in. "It's 'The Kathy.'"

"Sophie, my princess!" George picked Sophie up and spun her around. "I'm so glad my dingbat of a son hasn't scared you away."

"It'll take a crowbar, George."

Renee tipped her head to the side in examination of Kathy. "You're not what I expected."

Kathy looked down at the new clothes Sophie made her buy. The short, flowing violet skirt, fitted print V-neck top, and new heels were certainly not her norm. No, this was an outfit that required talking into, even if it still bordered on the traditional.

"I…ah…went shopping with Sophie…and…."

"Oh," Renee stated, as if understanding. "She can talk a hungry carnivorous beast into becoming a vegetarian."

"I cannot!"

Detective Owen cleared his throat. "Excuse me. Miss Smith, if you're going to be staying a bit longer, we can have that talk now."

Dave seethed. "You can wait until tomorrow."

"Relax, Dave. I'm more than capable of taking care of myself. Tomorrow, Detective Owen," she grumbled.

George stepped forward. "What's the problem, officer?"

"There was a little disturbance here," Dave told his father while glaring at Owen.

"I'm investigating—" Owen began.

"Harassing," Jake mumbled.

"—a lead I was presented a few weeks ago."

Renee crossed her beefy arms. "And what does that have to do with my boys?"

"Nothing, Ma. Nothing at all," Dave interjected.

"Then why is this officer questioning you?"

"Detective." Owen stated while reaching out a hand for a shake. "Detective Owen."

George rocked back on his heels, something Kathy had seen Jake and Dave do numerous times. "What does a detective have to do with what happened here tonight?"

"Nothing," Dave grumbled.

"I was at the station when the call came in. Thought I'd come down and help."

"Harass," Jake repeated.

Owen spared him a glance. "I'm being thorough."

"And we can appreciate that but why exactly are you interested in my sons?" George wanted to know.

Owen puffed out his hefty chest. "What I questioned your son about has nothing to do with this incident. As far as I can tell, those guys were causing a ruckus and Mr. Sanders, Dave, used unnecessary force to restrain one of them."

"I didn't restrain him." Dave's face turned a deep shade of red and Kathy could have sworn she saw steam come from his ears.

"No. You used undue force."

"Detective Owen," Renee stepped to the officer, "are you accusing my son of something?"

"No. I never said that."

"How about implying he did something wrong? Other than using what you call, 'undue force.'"

"He knocked a man out, Mrs. Sanders—"

"And you don't believe what? There was a good enough reason?"

"The men said they were getting ready to leave when they were jumped by both your sons," Owen insisted.

"Liars," Kathy mumbled.

"This is their restaurant. If someone is causing a problem, they have a right to ask them to leave." Renee stood firm, defending her boys.

"Yes, ma'am. But they don't have the right to—"

"Defend themselves and their customers?" Renee asked.

"Yes, they have a right. But if there is a problem then they should have called the police right away."

"Which was done," Dave added.

"After you knocked that man out." Owen pointed to the guy with the ice pack on his face. "You seem to like finding trouble, Sanders."

Kathy watched with amazement as both elder Sanders turned on the detective. The devotion, trust, and love seemed to over-power anything Owen tried to prove.

"It's time for you to leave, Detective Owen. Or I'll file a stay-away order on you. We understand each other?" Renee demanded.

Owen looked at Jake, Sophie, Dave, and Kathy. "I'll being see-ing all of you tomorrow," he said before walking away.

Dave let out a long, slow breath, "I'm gonna bring Kathy home, and rest my arm 'cause it's throbbing. Plus I'm hungry and pissed off. Jake, can you close up?"

"Yeah, Dude. All's good here."

"Thanks. Ma, Dad, I love you. You're welcome to stay at my house as long as you don't interrogate me."

"We would never do such a thing," Renee said, fluttering her lashes at her son.

"Oh, never you!" Dave hugged his father and mother good-bye then walked out the door before Kathy even made the move to get her jacket.

A little muddled she looked around. "Ah, Sophie, I guess Dave's bringing me home. Renee, George, it was…umm…an interesting first meeting. I hope we can…ummm—"

"Don't get nervous, honey." George wrapped his lean arms around her then picked Kathy up clear off the floor in a hug. "We can't wait for supper tomorrow night."

"Supper?" she asked in confusion.

Chapter 7

Dave slammed the door shut to his borrowed car as he waited for Kathy. He could only imagine what was going through Kathy's head right now. Loser, criminal. God he hoped she didn't quit the Lion. He didn't want her to do that, they were just starting to get to know each other. She always talked about how nice she found him. What a good guy he was. He could see it now—her finding out he wasn't this stand-up guy, and then wanting nothing to do with him. Isn't that how it always happened? He would meet a woman he liked, and who liked him back, then his criminal record would be revealed. Mostly by accident. But sometimes, when it seemed as if it might be a serious relationship, he would confess. What a mistake that always turned into. Nonetheless Dave had promised himself that honesty was what he would live by, and if a woman couldn't accept his past, then she couldn't accept him.

Kathy slid into the passenger seat with her cell in her hand.

"What's up?" he asked.

"Nothing." Her reply was short and he could tell she was upset with whoever had been on the phone.

"You sure?"

"Yeah." She turned to him with a smile. "Okay, boss, let's go."

He looked at her for a long moment, neither one saying anything to the other. "Well? You must have something to say to me after all of that," he finally asked.

Kathy visibly cringed. "I'm sorry, Dave."

Here it comes. The crash and disappointment. Just once, can't I be wrong? "For what?" he asked.

"I'm sorry but your parents kinda scare me."

He couldn't deny how relieved he felt to hear her unexpected reaction. "They frighten me too."

With a small smile and mesmerizing eyes, Kathy leaned toward him. "I think your mother scared Detective Owen, too."

Leaning into her Dave could feel the sexual energy sparking in the air around them. He eyed her lips before looking into her eyes. "She can terrify the devil."

"Absolutely," Kathy whispered.

Their faces were so close. Dave caressed his nose to hers. "She likes you."

"Really? How can you tell?" Kathy tipped her head ever so slightly up, and he accepted her invitation.

With his lips traveling along her jaw, he told her. "Ma would have focused on you instead to make sure you're not going to break my heart."

"Oh, Dave." He tugged on her earlobe with his teeth. "I'm worried about mine."

"Good." Pulling back he gently touched his lips to hers. *Slow,* he reminded himself. *Take your time.* When he slid his tongue into her mouth Kathy's body tightened under the arm he had wrapped around her. She fisted her fingers in his hair and tried to take them both deeper, wilder, but he wouldn't allow it. Keeping the kiss gentle he took his time tasting, all the while memorizing the smooth texture of her lips. "You're so beautiful, Kathy," he said, against her mouth.

"Come inside."

He sat back to look at the woman he hoped would someday be his. He'd known from the instant they met in the Lion's manager's office when Sophie had worked there. Kathy was the kind of woman he wanted to spend the rest of his life with. But he couldn't tell her, not yet. Not when there were still things she needed to know about him and him about her.

He pulled into her apartment building parking lot then turned to her. "You and I... the first time we make love, it's going to be special. Not just a grope fest."

"There's nothing wrong with those." Kathy teased with a hand caressing up his thigh.

"Nope, there isn't as long as you're both getting something great out of it." He took her hand in his and started to gently rub his thumb over the back of it. "I want to make you squirm and hear you scream out my name. I don't want the chance to catch our breath— no downtime, only passion." He began to put more pressure on the friction of her thumb pad. "When you come that first time, I want it in my mouth. My God, Kathy, I can't even get close to telling you how much I need you because I'm so overwhelmed by you."

"Oh, Jesus," she whispered. "Tell me more. Tell me how."

"I want to take you in every position possible with long slow strokes." His eyes burned into hers, and when he moved his hand under her skirt he found her moist. Gently he glided his middle finger in small circles over the dampness when he heard her breath shutter then gasp as he applied pressure. "I'd love to taste you now." He brought his hand to his mouth and sucked on the finger that he just teased her with.

"Dave?" Her body slithered lower in her seat, her eyes wide and filled with passion.

"Yes?"

"I feel like I'm going to explode. Pleasssse," she pleaded.

"Please what?"

"Come inside."

Hopping out of the car, they both raced to her apartment door. Dave stood behind her, his hands on her breasts, as she unlocked it. He then pushed her inside, and flung her around so she faced the closed door.

Gliding his hands up her sides and then her arms, he brought them above her head and cuffed them there with one hand.

"The things I've dreamed about doing to you," he whispered. Leisurely he unzipped her skirt and let it float to the floor. "Nice," he told her while tracing the V-string panties with a finger. "I'd always imagined you wore something like this. Keep your hands up."

Letting go, Dave lifted her shirt while letting one finger from each hand trail along her skin. Her body arched, trying to escape the gentle touch.

"I can't decide if that tickles or not," she told him, giggling breathlessly.

With her shirt gone, he began tracing the tops of her breasts. "What do you feel?"

"Everything. Don't stop."

"You don't have to worry about that." He hooked a finger under the front of her bra and lifted up, exposing her breasts. "Keep your hands up," he told her when they started to slide down the door. "Tell me what you want."

"I want this."

"Be more specific." He could feel her breath pulling in and out of her chest. He knew he could have her but this wasn't about him. He wanted to please her, show her what it was like to be taken care of. He didn't just want a quick lay. That's not what she deserved.

"I want you."

"To what?" he asked, while rolling her nipples between his fingers. Her knees went weak and Dave moved one hand to her stomach and one between her legs to keep her up. He couldn't wait to see her fly. Only in his dreams could he ever get close to her, now she was standing in front of him, practically naked and begging for release.

"I feel like I'm going to go crazy. I...I...can't think."

"Kathy, what do you want?"

"I want...."

He turned her around and with his lips to hers, abruptly hiked her up around his waist and pushed them both against the door. Deliberately he slowed the kiss, took his time with it so she would feel every sensation he brought to her while his hands kneaded her bottom. Every time Kathy tried to push him to go faster, rubbed her need against his, Dave would pull back and she'd murmur in protest.

"Make me yours. Please."

How could he say no to such a plea? He thrust her body farther up so he could travel kisses to one of her breasts. Once there he suckled and nipped at the erect peak until Kathy cried out and her body began to buck. As he moved to the next one, they slowly slid to the floor.

On his knees Dave buried his face between her legs. "You smell delicious. I can't wait to find out how you taste." He moved her panties aside and explored her with one finger.

"Oh!"

He licked his finger then reached up, beckoning her to taste. "Sweet. Just like you." She took the offering and suckled. "Wow, that's hot." With tender tugs Dave removed her panties. Once exposed he flicked his tongue over the sensitive swollen nub in hopes she would feel the same passion he was.

"Dave, you're killing me."

"No. I'm pleasuring you. Let go." He brought her to her knees and kissed her lips with violent impatience. She wrapped around him so forcefully he fell back against the floor.

He turned them so she could brace her hands on the door and moved her tasty center to hover over his mouth. "I'm living a dream." Blowing over her softly, Kathy's body trembled. Next he tenderly teased her lips with his tongue and she jolted. "Come down here," he commanded, and brought her to his mouth. Instantly she cried out. Dave used one hand to hold her up and the other to tease. He found himself as excited as her, and knew he would lose his own control in his pants the moment she did in his mouth.

Quicker and quicker his tongue moved over her. Three fingers deep, he felt the velvet walls tighten. Not wanting her to start thinking, he took her swollen morsel between his teeth. Kathy exploded. She rode him hard, coming again and again. Looking up Dave witnessed the most breathtaking woman he'd ever laid eyes on.

* * *

She'd never done that before. How could she look him in the eyes after what she'd just experienced? That is, if she could move from where she melted on the floor. Kathy's body involuntarily shook. Damn, she felt good. No wonder people got addicted to sex.

"What?" Dave asked, from beside her.

"Huh?"

"You said something."

She blinked at the ceiling. "I did?"

He giggled. "Yup. About addiction and sex."

"Did you just giggle?" Turning on her side, she regarded the fully clothed man beside her.

"Probably. You seem to be able to do all sorts of exciting things to me."

"To you!" She lay back down and stared at nothing of interest. "Dave, that was...."

"Incredible."

"I've never felt anything like that before. Wow. It feels so wrong, though. How can you say 'incredible' when you got nothing out of it?"

"Sweetheart. This isn't only about receiving. You can get just as much pleasure from giving."

She would have to think that over. Giving had never brought her much joy. Of course receiving hadn't either until just a few minutes ago. "Guess we'll have to try that some time."

In a flash, Dave rolled on top of her. "You'll enjoy it. I promise."

"Stay the night." She reached for his face and brought his lips down to hers. The lingering taste of herself brought on a wave of desire so severe it was jolting.

"I have to get back home to my parents. Plus I need a shower and a change of underwear."

"Underwear? Why in the world would you need that?"

His smile looked devilish. "I came too."

"Really?"

"Really. You do that to me, Kathy Mae Smith."

"I... how? I didn't touch you. I mean... I didn't do anything."

"You don't have to." Dave gathered her close. "Watching you is such a turn-on, you have no idea!"

When he massaged her breast, she leaned into it. "Sure you don't want to stay? This was my first real experience with this sort of thing and I'll need a lot more practice." Did she really just say that? But instead of cowering, she looked at him with determination. She loved the feelings Dave brought out of her.

"No...yes."

"What's the worst that could happen?" Kissing his neck, nibbling on his ear, her hands roamed his body. Her power to possess him grew more intoxicating with each of his moans. She wanted so much more than this quick fling in her doorway. "Could I persuade you into staying?"

"Yes." His voice sounded intense, his breathing deeper as she undid the button and zipper of his jeans.

"I've been wanting to see what you have down here."

"Kathy."

"Wow, Dave. This looks to be very restricting." What was she doing? She'd never seduced a man before. Yet here she was doing it without a skilled plan.

"What are you doing, Kathy?" He lifted his hips when she started to tug down his jeans.

"I'm going to give and you're going to receive."

She leaned down and with a flick of her tongue, heard Dave's hissed breath.

"That feels great."

With her confidence growing, Kathy explored some more. She glided her mouth down as far as she could go and...

"Wait. Wait."

"Did I do something wrong?" She'd just die if he said yes so close to the beginning of her journey.

"Oh, no. No, Muffin." He cupped her chin, kissed her then arched himself to the side to search out the back pocket of his jeans. "My parents." With a huff, he flipped his phone open. "What?"

Kathy smacked his chest. "Be nice."

By the moonlight seeping in through her windows Kathy saw him wink at her. "Mom, I'll be home in a little bit…Yes, I'm still with Kathy…I guess I could. Kathy, you're gonna come to the belated Easter dinner tomorrow night, right?"

Dinner? "I…."

"She's stuttering so I'm taking that as a yes…No, I'm not pushing her into anything she doesn't want to do…Mom, please don't do that…" He cupped the back of Kathy's head and with the phone still to his ear, Dave kissed her brainless. "What? Yeah, you are interrupting something…No, I'm not being fresh."

"Yes, you are," Kathy whispered in horror and began to get up.

"Oh, no you don't," he told her and pulled her back down to him. "Mom, I need to let you go. I'll be home soonish. Love you." Hanging up the phone he turned to her with narrowed eyes. "Where do you think you're going?"

"I…you told her we're having sex."

"No, I didn't."

Kathy wanted to pull her hair out. Men could be so dense. "Yes, you did."

He sat up and pulled his shirt off. "I can't help what goes on in her imagination, Kathy. Just like I can't help wanting to feel your hands on me again." He took one of hers and wrapped it around his hard shaft. Kathy hardly noticed. She was too busy looking at Dave's toned chest covered in tattoos. Her mouth went dry.

"You're a bad boy, aren't you, Dave?"

"Kathy, my love…" He kissed her hard then lay back on the

floor with his hands behind his head, an open invitation for her to feast. "You have no idea."

"Tell me what to do. Tell me what you want."

"Nope. You're running this show."

Tentative, she fastened her mouth around him. Ascending down the thick temptation, she found herself lost in the domination she felt. He groaned when she touched him with her fingers then arched when her mouth explored the sacks below. When she worked him beyond any reasonable thought, he exploded in her mouth.

Again they lay speechless in the moonlit entryway.

"Wow," Dave finally spoke. "You have a gift. And you can use that on me any time."

She couldn't help but laugh when he wiped the sweat from his brow. "Really? Not just trying to butter me up for your leaving?"

"I don't want to leave. Gosh, you're beautiful in the moonlight."

Kathy snorted before her focus turned to his chest. "Tell me what these mean." She traced a finger along the tattoos stretched across his torso, abdomen, and arms. "I never knew all these were here. Where'd you get them?" He got quiet and even in the little bit of light, Kathy could see him pondering how to answer her question. "Dave?"

"I got this one." He pointed at the large menacing devil on his right shoulder. "And this one." The angel on his left shoulder. "In jail."

He watched her, looking for some reaction he seemed sure would come. "Did they hurt?"

"You're not gonna ask why I was in jail?"

"No. Unless you want me to." For some reason it really didn't seem important. As if anything he'd been in there for wasn't as bad as the fear she saw in his eyes.

"I'm … speechless."

"Well, there's no reason for that. Did they hurt?" she asked again.

Dave took the hand tracing his ink and kissed it. "I have a record."

"Me too. Actually it's a forty-five recording of the original *Muppet Movie* theme. I hear it's worth money." He laughed and she realized she liked the sound, knowing she brought the humor out of him.

"Yes, they hurt."

"I have a phoenix on my left butt cheek. Sophie and I got them at the same time."

"Sophie has a tattoo?"

"Yup. On her shoulder blade."

His hand slowly caressed her side, sliding up until it cupped the back of her neck. He kissed her. "I'm gonna have to see that ink in a lot more light, Kathy."

"It's not like I have a whole lot on."

"I might just have to rethink my—" The vibration of his phone interrupted his words. "Damn phone!" He felt for it in the dark and Kathy watched his irked expression by the dim phone light. "What!"

Things couldn't be any more perfect. No, actually they would be if Dave stayed the night. But she understood why he couldn't. His parents were waiting for him and probably wanted a better explanation to what they had walked in on tonight at the bar and what was going on with Detective Owen.

Flopping on her bed face up, Kathy stared at her ceiling. *He did it.* Dave gave her an orgasm and promised to make it happen again and again. It was everything she dreamed it would be and so much more. She rolled over and snuggled into her pillow. A moment before sleep took her she thought, *I could get used to this.*

Chapter 8

Renee clapped her hands together. "I'm so excited. I haven't seen Mitch in forever!" Taking a long sip of her martini, she leaned back on Dave's couch and threw her feet up on the ottoman. "When did you find out?"

"While I was at Kathy's." Mitch was a longtime friend. They'd met years ago when his family took their summer vacations at the same place Dave's parents did. "He said he'll be here sometime in the next two days. He'll find out for certain tonight."

Dave busied himself with supper. Cooking had, in much the same way as his brother, become his refuge. Being able to throw all those tastes together and make them into something great was the easy part. It was the making sure nothing burned that got him every time.

George looked over Dave's shoulder and down at the frying pan. "Maybe you could use more oil."

"Maybe you'd like to cook your own food," he teased.

"No need to be testy with your dad," Renee commented from the sofa.

"HA. Mom, it's eleven at night. I'm tired and instead of

sleeping, I'm cooking a meal for the two strays that showed up at my place." He turned and winked at his mother then rolled his shoulder in the sling while George leaned against the counter next to him.

"Tsk-tsk. You should be excited we're here," his father told him.

"Why?"

"We can tell you want to know what we think of Kathy," George told him.

Dave concentrated on the onions in the pan. *Probably should get the meat in here before they fry to ashes.* "Make yourself useful and hand me the ground meat."

George held the plate of meat above his head and away from Dave. "Admit you like the girl."

Placing the blandest look he could on his face and with one hand on his hip, Dave answered, "I like the girl and she's helped me a lot while I've been in this damn sling. Now give me the meat or you're cooking the rest yourself."

George lowered it while studying Dave's eyes. "That was too easy, don't you think, dear?"

"Way too easy. He's hiding something," Renee informed her husband jauntily.

"I'm hiding nothing. You wanted to hear it. I said it." The meat fell in the pan with a good-natured plop and began to sizzle.

"George, my love?"

"Yes, Goddess?"

"I'm in hell," Dave said aloud to himself but couldn't help the grin that split his lips.

"I think our son is in love."

"Sugarplum, you may be right. Is that what you're hiding, Dave?" With both hands George took his son by the head and examined his eyes. "Looks like he could use more sleep."

"I'd be sleeping if I wasn't cooking and being harassed." Despite all his attempts, Dave couldn't keep the laugh in. His parents were truly crazy in such a fun way.

"Sweety?" Renee pulled herself off the couch. "Check his teeth."

"What?" Dave pulled away from his father. "I'm going to bed. You two wacky old people can finish your own meal and clean up after yourselves."

"Who would have thought?" George asked his wife. "That our oldest would be such a nitpicky shit."

"Why couldn't you both stay at Jake's? He has more room," Dave baited with his hand on his hip.

Renee kissed her son's cheek. "We wanted to help you out. You know, with the bad arm and all."

"Then why am *I* cooking?"

"Well, that's how we're helping you out," George pointed out. "We know you're not going to let us touch anything or take care of you, so we're going to let you do it for us."

Both his parents' smiles broadened. "That sounds pathetic, you know. And awfully like you're taking advantage of me."

George shrugged. "Maybe. But you're not stuck with Jake and Sophie. They offered to let us stay at their place and they would stay here."

"I don't think so!" Dave returned to the stove and stirred the meat. "They were terrible to live with!"

"See," Renee pointed out. "We're doin' you a favor."

As Dave watched his father slowly sit at the kitchen table, it reminded him that these two special people weren't getting any younger and how glad he was they came to visit as often as possible.

"Okay," George announced. "I'm going to ask about the big purple elephant in the room."

With a wooden spoon Dave chopped at the ground meat with a vengeance. "Detective Owen asked about some old drug contacts. I don't know where those people are, if they're alive, and I don't really care. I'm clean."

"Dave." Renee wrapped her son in her arms. "We are so proud of you. We know you're clean and have nothing to do with those people."

"Well, he's sniffing around." Dave shrugged his shoulders as if the whole ordeal didn't bother him, which was far from the truth. With a history like his there was always someone suspicious of him. "He'll get bored of watching me wipe down counters."

George studied his beer with consideration. "What will you do if he starts hanging around the Lion?"

"Serve him."

Renee shook her head. "It's been so long. No one should be harassing you."

"The only people doing that are the two of you." Dave pulled his mother back into a hug and kissed the top of her head. "It's okay. They can check the books. I have nothing to hide."

"What about Kathy?" George wanted to know.

"What about her?" Dave went back to the meat that now swam in grease yet still seemed to be burning.

"Do you have anything to hide from her?"

"The both of you are dreadful people. Here's your son cooking dinner for his starving parents in the middle of the night, and all you can do is drill me. Can you at least wait until the morning?"

Dave shook his head when his mother said, "George, we can start asking him questions in thirty minutes. It'll technically be tomorrow and he'll have calmed down."

"Impossible. Both of you!" Dave tossed the seasoning in with the meat, along with water, noodles, and milk, then turned the flame down to simmer. "Okay guys, I'm going to bed."

"So Kathy doesn't know."

His mother's sad eyes grabbed at his soul—a reminder that all his parents wanted was what was best for him. "You make it sound as if I tell the women I date all my nasty secrets, right away. It's a fine line. If you tell them too fast, they run. If you tell them too late, they say you're dishonest. What do you think I should do?"

Renee sat next to her husband at the table. "What do you want to do?"

"I told her I've done time. She really seemed all right with it. Kathy's coming to dinner tomorrow. What more could I ask for?"

George stood and grabbed some plates from the cabinet, setting them on the counter. "I want my boys to be able to have happy lives. It's the only thing your mother and I have ever wanted."

"I am happy."

"Alone, without Jake?" his father asked.

"Dad, I'm not alone. Are you going through some kind of crisis or something?"

"No, Dave, your father isn't going through a crisis. He's worried."

"Why? Because I don't have a woman? Come on, guys." His father suddenly looked tired, the lines on his face deep from worry and the perpetual light in his eyes just a bit dimmer. He even seemed to have lost a few pounds. "What's going on?"

"You know what's going on, son? I'll tell you what's going on! My boys have had to fight for everything they've got. Yes, you two have gotten into your share of trouble. What boy doesn't?

But you've become good men. Why can't everyone just leave you alone?"

"Sweetheart, remember your blood pressure," Renee reminded George.

"I don't give a flying you-know-what about that!" his father yelled.

"Well you should. Dad, park it." Dave guided his father by the arm and made him sit. "First of all Jake and I are not a mess. He's a very happy man who found a woman who can put up with his crap. She's the best thing to ever happen to him and because of all the other crazy stuff he's been through, he appreciates her. Second I'm not lonely without him. Just because he has a chick doesn't mean I'm now lost. I have friends, I date, and I have my business. Yes, I was more trouble than most parents could handle. But the two of you stuck in there. You believed in me when I was at my worst. You didn't write me off even when I was doped up, stealing, lying, running, or incarcerated. I can't say I would've done the same. I'm here because of the both of you.

"You want to know about Kathy? There's not much to say. Up until a week ago she didn't seem interested. But then something changed and I'm so happy it did. We'll see where it goes. For now I'm going to bed. Enjoy your late-night meal, get some sleep, and stop worrying." Dave kissed his mother and father on the head. "I love you."

"We love you too, son."

Yes, you do. Dave smiled. And for some inexplicable reason a past moment of his darkest days flashed before him. He had gotten out of the hospital and was staying at his parents'—not a druggy friend's pad or crashing at the strip bar he had called home more often than not.

George had come into Dave's room and caught him cutting

and weighing dope to be sold. Livid was an understatement to what Dave saw in his father's eyes. When the argument began they were in each other's faces screaming.

"You're throwing your life away for those lowlife friends. They're not worth it," George screeched.

Dave pushed his father out of the room and against the hallway wall. "You don't know dick. Now get the hell out of my way."

His father's sorrowful eyes bore into him. "Fine. Leave. But the next time you're lying in the hospital, dying or dead, I'll still be there. That's what family does, love unconditionally."

His loving father had successfully planted the seed of guilt; and instead of being remorseful Dave responded by stealing his car but not before striking the older Sanders in the face.

Dave had been so angry at what his father said. He didn't deserve to be forgiven. The apple had fallen so far from the tree that it actually rolled down the hill and into a bog of dung to rot.

George's Chrysler had started with a roar while Dave watched through the windshield as his father lumbered to his feet. The look of disappointment George showed toward his son was so evident and painful that it caused Dave to question himself. *How could I have done that to the man who stood by me when I needed him the most?*

That moment would stick in Dave's mind forever. His father bleeding by his son's hand. What a monster, what an animal— what a wrong road traveled. It would be two weeks before they were face to face again.

"*I don't deserve forgiveness* but I'm willing to try to make up for the bullshit I've caused," Dave swore to them.

And that's what he'd done. Donations of money and his time toward any cause he believed in. Volunteering at shelters and food banks to help those less fortunate and desperate for help. Even speaking at recovery meetings in hopes he could inspire others. All of this he did for his parents and very little for himself.

* * *

"Sophie, I know it's late. But I woke up and needed to talk to someone."

"Is something wrong?"

"No, no. I'll call back tomorrow."

About to hang up, Kathy heard Sophie yell, "You hang up and I'll come speeding over."

"You sure?" She couldn't wait to share the news. Like a teen crush come true, Kathy began to talk and found she couldn't stop. "Because it's fine. Even though I really need to talk to someone right now and I'd like it to be you. Oh, no. Is Jake there? Because I'd rather he didn't know what we're about to talk about. Embarrassing."

"He can't hear you, Kathy. What's wrong?"

"Something's wrong with Kathy?" Jake asked.

"No. Go back to sleep, Jake. Hold on, Kathy, I'm going in the other room."

Kathy wiped her sweaty palms on her pajama pants while her heart jackhammered. "I should have called earlier but I was too busy arguing with myself about calling. This is so…so…."

"Kathy?"

"Yes?"

"Does this have to do with Dave or the guy at the bar?"

"Dave, of course. Do you think I'd be so worked up if it was about that dirtball? Please! I can take care of jerks like him. Although I have to say seeing Dave punch him out was totally a turn-on."

"I know. I saw you grab him."

"So…"

"Yes?"

"Is oral sex sex?" At the silence on the other end of the phone Kathy began biting her nails. A nasty habit she hoped to some-day grow out of.

"Umm. President Clinton said it wasn't but, yeah, I believe it is. Kathy, what happened between you and Dave?"

"Oh…my…God! I had an orgasm right against my front door! I'm totally addicted! I want to call him and make him come back so we can do it all again but I'm afraid he'll say no. Or worse! His parents will answer. 'Hi, this is Kathy. Can Dave come over and play dentist with me? I have a cavity that needs filling.' Can you imagine?" She could hear her friend's hysterics on the other end of the receiver. Knowing how odd the situation was, Kathy couldn't help but laugh, too. "You know this isn't funny."

"Oh, it is. It is!"

"It was so…so…erotic. I mean, he has a way with telling me what to do and—"

"Whoa! He tells you what to do? Like, makes you do things?"

"No, not like that. You know…in the kinky way."

"Nice!"

"I totally forgot about being nervous and *wow*, it was incredible!"

"Maybe you're a submissive," Sophie suggested.

"A what?" She'd heard the word before but in her excitement couldn't seem to bring the definition to mind.

"Maybe you like to be dominated?"

Did she like to be? What kind of question was that? Of course she didn't! What woman in her right mind liked to be bossed around? She was a fully successful woman who didn't need someone telling her what to do. Especially in bed. "Tell me you want this." Dave's words echoed in her brain.

"Oh, no! I think I am. Is that okay? Is there something wrong with me?"

"Kathy, calm down. It's okay. This might actually be why it took so long."

"I didn't even think. I mean, I didn't even try to stop him. No hesitation. Nothing. I was a total slut and loved every minute of it. I'm a whore."

"You're not a whore. You just had the most incredible sex of your life and enjoyed it. Right?"

"We didn't have sex! That's what I don't understand. Am I going to be able to handle it when we finally do 'it'? And what if I don't orgasm then? What if it's the sex part that my body doesn't react to? I'm a miserable mess." Her body became a jumble of nerves the moment Dave left. It caused her to pace nonstop in hopes of burning off some of the crazy energy their sexual encounter gave her. "How am I going to face him tomorrow?"

"Like you do every other day. You'll say 'hi' and go to your office."

"How did you do it? Work with Jake and not sleep with him?"

"It was different, Kathy. Jake didn't want to sleep with me."

"Right. I forgot about that." She started to chew on her nails again then whispered, "He's got a really nice dick, Sophie."

"Umm...I'm happy for you? Congratulations? Umm...gross. You might be talking about my future brother-in-law."

"Sorry. He has these really awesome tattoos across his chest."

"You saw them? I haven't gotten a look at them yet. He keeps them pretty covered."

"Why?"

"You'll have to ask him."

"He told me he got them in jail." Kathy waited a beat in hopes that this was the information Sophie had held back from her. "Maybe that's why."

"Probably," Sophie answered.

"He shouldn't be embarrassed. They're really nice. At least they looked that way in the sliver of light I could see them with."

"How do you feel about him doing time? I mean, does it change any of your feelings?"

Pensive, Kathy remained silent for a moment while she tried to figure out a way to say "yes" without sounding slutty. "Truth?"

"I'd prefer it. And so would Dave."

"I know he must have done something awful but look at all he's accomplished. I've never been into men with a past but with Dave it doesn't seem to matter at all. I'm so confused. It turns me on, Soph. When I saw those tats and knew where he had gotten them, I wanted to taste every part of that man's body. It's so wrong, and so right."

Sophie's laughter rang through the phone. "It's not wrong. Enjoy every orgasm you have with him."

"But even though he's dominant, he's so gentle. It drove me crazy. Even when it felt like he was rushing, he seemed to be going too slow. Wow, it was incredible!"

"So now what are you going to do?"

"Take a very cold shower and hope I don't make a dingy of myself tomorrow at work and tomorrow night at dinner. Please say you're going to be there," Kathy pleaded. "That it's going to be all of us. Together. In a public place."

"Yes, Jake and I will be there. There's nothing to worry about."

"What if his parents know what happened between us? I mean, I think they already do because they called in the middle of it but I'm afraid they're going to see it on our faces. Maybe I should cancel."

"Kathy, you're not children and Dave's parents know he's had sex. And the different variations there are of it. You'll be fine."

Kathy dropped her head in her hand. "I think I'm going to be sick."

"Calm down."

"My body is still trembling. My head is dizzy. What's wrong with me?"

"What a lucky girl! You're still having an orgasm"

"What? They can last this long?"

"Hell, yeah. When done right. Have any brandy in the house?"

"Yeah." Kathy jumped off the couch and quickly crossed her legs while standing. "The tickle between my legs won't stop. Should I drink the whole bottle?"

"Of liquor? No. A couple shots and a cold shower."

"Has this ever happened to you?"

"No. I mean they've lasted an hour or so after but not this long."

Kathy's eyes grew wide with concern. "Should I call a doctor if it doesn't stop?"

Sophie snickered. "No. You should call Dave and tell him to get his ass over there."

"You're right. Okay. I'm gonna drink, shower, and dream of Dave. Goodnight, Sophie!"

Kathy hung up before her friend could answer. Erotic fantasies of Dave and insecurities about her abilities to please a man mocked her. Was she good enough? Did she want a relationship? Could she handle one? But even as she pushed her insecurities aside, the divine tremors she had been rejoicing slowly morphed into turbulent shakes. Tears rushed down her face as she dropped to the floor. Anchoring one hand to the arm of the couch she hoped it would prevent her soul from being swept away and into misery. But pain, contempt, and a child's lost virtue tore at her in an attempt to free itself from the shackles that she had confined it with.

Todd had hit her so hard in the stomach that she never thought she'd be able to breathe again.

"No!" She raged, even as her body insisted on curling into a tight fetal ball. *Don't go back there. I need to... I need to...* The murky depths of her past began to pull her down to a world of hopelessness.

Must she continuously relive this? She wanted to bask in the joy of Dave, not tarnish it with her past.

Todd then grabbed her by her hair and dragged her to the bathroom.

She thought she had finally gotten over this. Hadn't she confronted Todd? Why did this always have to happen whenever there was a glimmer of hope, an inkling of a future? Terror and doubt were persistent in reminding her that these things could only be hers from a distance.

"You're going to learn that I'm in charge. Me." Todd then tossed her into the bathtub and turned the shower on, the water was ice cold. "Strip!"

The fractured truth echoed this nasty joke in her mind, and reminded her: *This is your reality. Why do you ask for more when you know you can't have it? Never have, and never will.* For she'd been taught at a very young age how undeserving of it she was. Selfish people don't get happily ever afters.

"You're a selfish little bitch and no one will want you except me. Now wash!" He handed her a scrub brush. Clumps of hair began to clog the drain as Karma rinsed and scoured her body.

"I didn't mean it. I didn't realize I did it," she pleaded.
"And now you'll make up for it."

Todd raped her twice that night because looking at a grocery store clerk wasn't something she should do. After years of therapy and countless setbacks, Kathy finally understood she hadn't deserved that beating, or any of the others that followed. Kathy also realized that she would never comprehend why her parents knew and did nothing about it.

Weeping harder didn't seem possible. So instead Kathy curled up on her living room floor and wept until a fretful sleep took her.

Chapter 9

Dave whistled while practically skipping into the Hungry Lion. Kathy would be there in an hour so he had to get as much done as possible. Staring at her, touching her, and being an all-around pain in the butt was what he planned on doing. Laughing at himself he unlocked the back door. She was perfect, everything he could have hoped for and never dreamed he could have. The beautiful eyes, the soft skin, and the way her body yielded and melted into his. No one had ever touched her the way he did last night. The mere thought of her low throaty moans made Dave's body stir. He'd be her first—the one to show her the sexy woman she truly was. And yet he couldn't help but think of the women in his past. The ones who said they were okay with the mistakes he'd made in his life and actually thought it was sexy. Oh, it had always started out great. The sex was good, the nights out were fun, but then the girls would realize he wasn't who he used to be and they would get bored and leave. And that was the ones who stayed and weren't trying to "reform" him when he already was. Dave shook his head at the thought, *those girls were the worst*. He really hoped Kathy wasn't like the others; she sure didn't seem to be.

Dave stopped for a moment and stood in the middle of the bar while he processed the magnitude of what had transpired between them. The black sticky ink of doubt rewrote the dreams he'd written, then covered his future hopes for him and Kathy with doubt. What if she decided he wasn't the one for her? Too much baggage.

A banging sounded on the front door knocked Dave out of his qualm. "We're closed!" he yelled to the figure behind the stained-glass door window.

"I know!"

Dave unlocked the door as quick as he could and flung it open to reveal his oldest and closest friend. "Mitch, you dumbass, you were supposed to call when you arrived."

"Yeah, but business pulled me here early so I thought I'd take a chance and stop in since we haven't been able to do our get away, ogle girls, and drink lots of beer vacations."

They shared a brotherly hug. "Well, if you hadn't moved to New York all those years ago we'd be able to do that right here during the summer. Damn, your hair's gotten gray. It must be the wife," Dave teased good-naturedly.

"And the baby. They're at the hotel sleeping so I figured I'd come over and bug you. So are you going to offer me a drink? Or do I have to get it myself?" Mitch joked.

"Yeah, yeah. Come on in." Dave relocked the door and gestured to the bar. "What can I get ya?"

"Soda."

"And?"

"Just soda. I'm going to be meeting with clients in a few hours." Mitch looked around the Hungry Lion Bar-n-Grill. "This really is a great place, Dave. How long has it been since we saw each other? Three years, since my wedding?"

"I guess you're right." Dave shook his head. "Time even flies when you're not having too much fun. How's being a family man?" Grabbing his friend a soda Dave pushed down the yearning he always experienced whenever he thought of Mitch, his wife, Simone, and their new daughter

"Great. Wonderful. Crazy. Hectic. Wouldn't change it for the world." Mitch's lips twitched. "Word is you've got your sights on a woman."

"Hmm...wonder who told you that."

"Don't blame me!" Jake came out of the back room yelling, and then extended a hand to Mitch for a shake.

"Well someone told him!" Dave shouted back.

Mitch turned his eyes on Dave. "It was your mom—this morning. She also said we're having a belated Easter supper tonight and you were in a hell of a wreck. How's the shoulder?"

Dave contemplated the glass of water in his hand while Jake stood crossed-armed behind Mitch. It was then that he knew why his old friend had come—Jake had asked him to. "The shoulder is good. Life is good. Why don't you speak what's on your mind, Mitch? You could have sent anyone here for that meeting."

"Nothing on my mind. I wanted to bring the baby up for you guys to meet," Mitch said innocently enough.

"Dave, that's no way to treat a friend you haven't seen in years. How about the three of us tie one on tonight? We'll get all crazy and shit." Jake slapped Mitch on the back.

"Jake, the last time you did that you were passed out naked on the office couch," Dave reminded him with a smirk.

"I wasn't passed out. I was sleeping after celebrating this one's baby being born."

Mitch chuckled. "So how's...." He trailed off as Kathy walked in. After swiveling around on the bar stool he gave her a dazzling smile. "Well, hello there. You guys always have the most beautiful women working here."

Dave cringed a little when Kathy turned a deep shade of red. "Mitch, this is Kathy, our new manager. Kathy, this is our old friend Mitch."

"Oh, I don't think he looks old," she teased while taking a step toward the man and extended a hand which Mitch brought to his lips.

"Pleasure to meet your acquaintance, Kathy."

Seeing through Mitch's pickup line and good-natured wit, she smiled bright with an edge of humor, while her voice mocked southern belle charm. "My, my. How did this smooth-talking man end up rustlin' with a couple derelicts like yourselves?"

Jake choked on his laugh while Mitch pulled an unsuspecting Kathy into his arms for a hug. "I like you already, Kathy."

"Hands off my woman, McCabe."

"I have my own and love her around the world and back. So, Kathy, how'd you end up working for these two?"

Kathy pressed her lips together before answering. "I'm best friends with Sophie."

"Ahhhh. *The* Sophie. So you're *The* Kathy."

"I suppose." She wanted badly to slide to the floor and then out of the room but something inside of her held strong. It told her she had nothing to fear from this stranger. "I guess Dave thinks I'm his woman." She gave Mitch a sly grin.

"I think we're going to have to correct that."

Mitch's eyes were kind while his smile calmed her nerves. "Yes," she said, feeling more daring. "Maybe we should tell him about us." Her eyes slid to Dave's as Jake's laughter rolled.

"You have a live one here, Dave," Mitch announced.

"Don't I know it." Gazing at her, Dave blew Kathy a kiss. "I think I'm going to kidnap her and run off to the Caribbean Islands. What do you say, Muffin?"

Kathy's quiet voice shuddered. "I…I think I'm going to have to think on that…I'm…I have a boss who's in need of some long overdue excitement, though. You should bring him."

"I'm not going anywhere with Dave, Jake announced, "especially on a romantic getaway."

"I'll go with ya, Dave." Mitch leaned over the bar and took his friend's face in his hands then laid a smacking kiss on him. "I've always lusted after you!"

"Aagggg! Get off of me! I want to go with her, not your flabby butt."

Kathy insides giggled up and then out. "Okay, enough fun, I'm off to my cave. Mitch, it was nice meeting you."

"You too." He surprised Kathy by giving her a peck on the cheek. "Behave," he told her.

"Psss," Jake countered. "She won't be if she keeps hanging with Dave."

"Maybe that's what I want," she countered before thinking and then put a hand over her mouth. "I…I guess he's already having an influence on me."

"And the plot thickens," Mitch teased. "I hope you don't mind but we men are gonna go out after dinner tonight, and we *are* going to drill Dave about you."

"Oh. Well, there's…I need to go."

"Leave her alone, Mitch." Dave took Kathy's hand and led her to the back office. "Sorry about that. Mitch is harmless and likes to get a rise out of me." He turned her into his arms as soon as they were inside the office. "I've been thinking about doing this again all night." His lips came to hers with serene patience. She fell with him when he guided her onto the couch. The feel of his body on top of hers, how they fit so flawlessly together, brought exhilaration and need bubbling to the surface.

"How do you do this to me? I don't understand," she told him. "I can't control anything when I'm around you." She moved her hands under his shirt. The smooth feel of his skin to the contrast of the delicate rise of his ink patterns transfixed her as she traced them with her fingers.

Dave nipped at the sensitive flesh of her throat as his hand moved up her body to cup her breast.

"I love when you kiss my neck."

Dave's teeth tugged at her ear while he fit his body securely between her legs. "You had amateurs before me. Men who were more concerned with their own needs than yours. I want to drive you. Make you so insane that you can't stop even when your body wants to." He kissed her harshly—a brutal promise of things to come. But Kathy's mind took a step back with caution bells singing loud and insistent. She tried to block out their negative tone and listen to the encouraging one that said she would gladly follow him wherever he led. That with him she felt secure, confident, and sexy, not fretful, used up, and drab. There wasn't any clumsiness when they were in each other's arms—only two people trying to put their trust in each other.

"How did this happen?" Her body deceived her skeptical mind by bowing under his.

"Luck. I'm the luckiest man in the world."

The truth of the statement was in his forceful stare, which caused a sudden, almost painful swelling in Kathy's chest. The tiny fiery ball ignited then bloomed into the most blissful wonderment she ever experienced. Surprised by the emotions and its origins, she realized it wasn't his hands discovering her body but his heart. The marvel of it consumed her while the scary reality drew her farther away from him.

"We need to stop," she said. His befuddled look made her wonder what his thoughts were. "I'm sorry. I don't want you to think I'm a tease. But let's be serious here."

"That might be a little hard with me lying on you." In an aggressive move, he sat up with his tongue in his cheek.

"Right." She slid herself up to a sitting position. "I want what's happening between us. Really I do...umm."

"So what's the problem?" His gravelly voice was edged with cynicism.

"I think we might be moving a little fast. That's all." *I'm doing this for us. It's the right thing to do. Step back a little before one of us hurts the other one.*

He narrowed his eyes as if to study her. "What's going on? Did you decide Mitch is the right man for you? Because he's married."

His attempt at humor gave her a smile. "I'm not interested in Mitch. *You* should know that by now."

"Sure about that?" He asked, with a raised brow.

"Oh, Dave." She cupped his face in her hands. "I've never felt what you make me feel and it's terrifying, yet exciting at the same time." She laughed at herself. "That sounds so ridiculous."

A wicked grin formed on his lips while he crawled across the couch to pull her slim body under his again. "I excite you?" He eyed the hand she pressed against his chest.

"Yes, but—"

"You're scared." How could she not be when he was terrified? "To death, Dave."

"Then I guess we'll start with a little necking in the car. Will your dad get upset?"

She laughed hard. "Oh, you need to meet my parents to get the full answer to that question."

"Are you inviting me to meet them?" he asked with a secret hope that she would.

"No," she said with pain present in her eyes.

"You don't want me to meet them, do you?" *You really don't want to take this relationship any farther than what we have right now?* he wanted to say to her.

"It's not that, Dave. They're just...I don't have the best relationship with them and when you do meet them," Kathy took a cleansing breath, "you'll understand."

Dave twirled a lock of her hair around his finger. She said, "When you *do* meet them," and that meant she was thinking about them having a future together. Excitement over her words moved his soul and gave him an optimism he hadn't felt in years. When he kissed her the whole world tilted and propelled his heart into hers. His hands slid over silken skin as he raised her shirt up for him to feast on her breasts. She answered his calling by fisting his hair in her hand and inciting him to not stop. Needing more Dave unzipped her slacks then sat back on his haunches to pull both pants and panties down below her bottom. When he replaced the cotton material with his hand Kathy ignited. Her mouth, hot and demanding, took his. It was all Dave could do to keep them from rolling onto the floor when she unbuttoned his jeans with haste then pushed them down so she could hold him in her hand. When those deft fingers began to massage him, Dave moaned her name. He wanted every single part of her to be his and not just her mind and body. No, he wanted her laughter, the blush that would come to her cheeks when he looked at her and winked but most of all he yearned to go to bed and then wake up next to her.

"Dave…"

"I know." Pulling back Dave gazed down at Kathy. "That was better than any backseat." Her eyes were heavy and her lips had a small smile.

"Yes, it was but we need to get to work and you have a friend waiting out in the restaurant for you."

When fun and laughter swept away from her eyes, Dave asked, "Tell me what's wrong, Muffin."

"I went and gave my report about last night." She stood from the couch and swiftly began fixing her clothes.

"And?" he asked while buttoning his pants.

"It seems like that detective is looking for something other than answers to what happened," she answered while averting her eyes from his.

Puzzled and a little taken aback, Dave probed, "What do you mean?"

"He kept bringing up all the break-ins and a drug bust that happened in the last few weeks."

Dave's back went up. "Did he ask you about me? Because, Kathy, I swear, I know nothing about any of that."

"No, no. I…." She faded off.

"So what's the problem?"

"I…there's other things. I just really hope you don't take this personally but I—"

"I understand." He stood, hurt evident on his face and in his words. "You need to do what's best for you." He ran his hands through his thick crop of hair. "Stepping back from you, honestly, Kathy, I'm not sure I can do that. What we've started here, it's not something that can just be stopped. I find myself so drawn to you."

"No, no, stepping back isn't it. Dave, there's so much more

going on than you and me. I know it's asking a lot but I need you to trust me and give me time and not ask questions."

Dave looked into her eyes where hurt and confusion were churning. "Okay. I can respect that. But don't think you're getting out of dinner tonight." He ran a finger down her nose.

"Well, that sucks," she teased with a flip of her hair. "And I was hoping to take a bubble bath and think about you all night."

"Oh…well, you can still do that." He pulled her in for a quick kiss. "We could always take the tubby together…tonight."

"One step at a time, Dave. For now you need to get your tight buns out there and work."

"God I love it when you're bossy," he told her as he walked out of the office whistling.

* * *

Dave leaned forward to wipe down the bar in front of him. Kathy's revelation irritated Dave, even hours later. Why couldn't she tell him what was bothering her? He was trustworthy and a good listener. It was a disappointing blow to know she didn't want to share her fears with him; that they hadn't reached that point in their relationship where they could tell each other anything. When Detective Owen walked into the bar area wearing civilian clothes, Dave's already rattled mood darkened. *The nerve of him. Why can't he just leave me alone?*

"Hey, can I get a Sam Adams?" Owen leaned a hefty hip on the bar stool.

"Coming up. Tap or bottle?"

"Bottle's fine."

He watched while Owen looked around. A small grin spread across the man's pudgy face when his eyes met Dave's.

"What?" he asked defensively.

"You did all right. Your parents are very proud of you."

"Owen, if you came in here to harass me, I'm gonna have to start reporting you."

Owen waved him off. "Naw. I'm here for a beer or two. Off duty. You didn't come in to give your side of the story this morning."

"Really?" Skeptical, Dave tried to be friendly. "That's why you're here?"

"No, I'm here for a friendly beer," Owen stated then took a swig of the bottle Dave had put in front of him.

Dave wiped at the bar and winked at a lady. "So, Owen. Wife, kids?"

"Why?"

"Just being sociable. Figured since you're bent on getting to know me by hanging around, I might as well get to know you. There's no motive." Dave held his hands up.

"Ex-wife."

"Ouch. Glad I don't have one of those. Hey, Jake." Dave greeted his brother with a "be nice" glare.

"What the hell you doing here, Owen?"

Owen swiveled on his seat to look at Jake. "Is that how you say hi to all your patrons?"

"Only the unwelcomed ones."

"Easy, Jake, he's here for a drink and *is* an officer," Dave told his brother.

"And to pin anything he can on you," Jake retorted.

"I'm not trying to pin anything on your brother, Sanders."

Jake's irritated voice had turned a few heads so Dave moved quickly. He couldn't have his place known for poor conduct. That wasn't good for business. Hell, with the guys they bounced out last night, and now this, a bad reputation was probably already starting.

"Go away, Jake. Now." His brother opened his mouth and then closed it. "I've got this."

Taking a long, measuring look at Owen, Jake said, "I owe my life to my brother. He's not who he used to be. Get it through your thick head."

"That's what everyone keeps saying. By the way, thank you for your service, Gunnery Sergeant." Owen took a sip of his beer. "And I'm not out to get your brother, no matter what you think. I only wanted a beer."

"Jake. Go."

"There's other places," Jake seethed through his teeth.

"Yup, but I picked this one."

Dave looked at them both and sighed heavily. There would never be peace in his life. "Jake, please."

"Fine," he snarled and stomped away.

"Sorry," Dave said to Owen. "My brother's a bit protective."

"It's not misplaced."

They stared at each other—whether for understanding or willing power over the other, Dave couldn't say. But he did know one thing, "The 'good cop' routine won't work with me, Owen. I've seen it too many times."

"Maybe I'm just looking to see what the other cops see."

"And maybe you're not." Dave moved down the bar. They were getting busy. Thankfully. It meant he wouldn't have to pay much attention to the unwanted customer. He could ignore Owen and have a good reason for it.

"Hey," Stuart called out to Owen, from his corner bar stool perch. "Leave Dave alone. He's a good guy."

"Stuart," Dave warned.

"What? This guy comes in harassing you and you stick up for him?" Stuart shook his head. "Louie told me about last night, you know, the fight? That you were a real prick."

Owen opened his mouth then closed it again, as if trying to figure out what to say.

"Well I think that's bullshit," Stuart went on.

"Stuart." Dave set a beer in front of his oldest patron. "Detective Owen deserves a little respect and didn't come here tonight to make trouble. Isn't that right?"

"Pfff. He smells like—"

"Exactly," Owen interrupted Stuart. "Just having a beer like you."

"I still say you smell." Stuart picked up his beer and grumbled. "Louie's right, we need rat traps in here."

Dave kept his retort to himself. No use getting the old man any more worked up than he already was. Besides Kathy came floating out of the back room and his tongue tied into knots. Her beauty only seemed to be magnified among the crowd. He wanted to run over, sweep her off her feet, and…and what exactly? Damn that woman jumbled his heart and his mind.

Filling another order Dave decided he knew what he wanted to do—take her away from all the ugliness that was filling up their world at the moment. Was that too much to ask? He supposed so because Owen, of course, noticed Dave's reaction to her appearance in the room.

"You've got it bad for Karma, eh?"

Puzzled he asked, "What?"

"The way you're looking at that girl. Karma?"

Dave wasn't sure if karma had anything to do with it but if it did, that would probably mean he wouldn't be getting the girl. The sides of his mouth pulled down. Maybe he should let her go before they got in too deep. After all she might be okay with the knowledge that he used to be a troublemaker but that didn't really matter much if it was going to cause conflict between her and her parents; wasn't that another problem he always had with the women he dated? The parents would find out and then convince their daughter that once a loser, always a loser.

Kathy turned those chocolate eyes on his and Dave knew he'd be miserable for the rest of his life without her but if it meant her happiness, so be it. He wouldn't push.

"Dave, I'm leaving for the day. Is there anything else you need?" Kathy asked.

Yeah. You. "No, I'm good."

Kathy took a ragged breath when her eyes fell on Owen. "Detective."

"Miss Smith."

Kathy looked over his shoulder. "Jake."

"Kathy."

"Louie," Kathy remarked.

"Kathy," Louie saluted with his drink.

"Dave," Dave said, feeling a little left out.

Jake's lips twitched. "Owen."

"Sanders," the detective answered.

"Okay, so now that we're all acquainted," Dave smirked, "what's next? How about a game of golf?"

"Never was good at it," Owen countered.

"How about target shooting?" Jake suggested, with a wiggle of his brows.

"Now that's just asking for trouble. Go away, Jake." The need to hit his brother came on sudden and strong.

"I personally like something quieter like…" Kathy rolled her eyes to the ceiling in deep thought. "Fishing. Never know what you'll find, or lose, in the water." All three men stared at her. "What?"

"Kathy." Dave leaned over the bar, cupped her chin in his hand, and kissed her soundly. "What a great idea. The two of us on a boat…*alone*. Fishing and enjoying each other," he added with a wink.

She pulled back suddenly, red faced and flustered. "I…ah. See you tonight at dinner." Then she sprinted out of the room.

Dave watched her leave. Man, he loved the look in Kathy's eyes when he flustered her. *Sexy.*

Chapter 10

Wait, wait, wait! Remember the time we filled my father's car with pine air fresheners?" Mitch asked with bubbling enthusiasm.

"You did not!" Simone, Mitch's wife exclaimed.

"We didn't just fill it, Mitch. We rubbed those nasty things all over his cloth seats. I smelled like a pine tree for days!" Dave reminded him.

Renee laughed loud and spoke louder. "As soon as that boy walked into my house, I knew he'd been up to something! Dad and I called your parents right away 'cause we'd known he'd been with you."

Mitch sat back in his dinner seat, threw an arm around the back of his wife's chair, and tsk-tsked the past antic. "He was sooo pissed. That car smelled until the day he turned it in."

Dave chuckled. "I think it was after that he told you to stop hangin' with me."

"No. That was after we disguised shaving cream as whipped cream and my mother put it on her ice cream."

"That's just mean and disgusting." Kathy tried to look

disappointed in Dave but couldn't quite pull it off. The chuckle rose in her throat until it finally released itself with a snort.

Simone laughed as she fed their baby more food. "You won't do nasty things like that will you, Emma?"

Dave chuckled as he watched Simone kiss her daughter on the head making Emma giggle and then squeal. Mitch sure had done right by himself—a beautiful wife and daughter, a successful architecture firm. There wasn't anything his friend had that Dave wouldn't have given his left arm to have.

When Mitch turned and kissed his wife, Dave thought. *"Good for him. He deserves to be happy."*

He and Mitch had met in between fourth and fifth grade while attending summer camp and soon became inseparable. Their antics had started there with cherry bombs in the outhouses. Of course they never got caught but Dave had a feeling his parents knew it was him and Mitch. Especially with all the things they did in the years following their buddying up.

"You think that was bad," Jake told Kathy. "You should have seen the look on our parents' faces when these two changed the locks on the house doors. They bought the same handles and everything! Mom and Dad couldn't get in."

"Mitch, remember that?" Dave said with nostalgia. Reminiscing on the harmless pranks he used to play on his and Mitch's parents was always a fun time. Plus their parents had been easy targets and good sports.

"I remember grounding you for a month." Renee smiled at her son. "Course I blamed it on Mitch."

"It was my idea, Mrs. Sanders," Mitch confessed.

George slapped him on the back. "And a good one at that."

"I miss your parents, Mitch," Renee said with a sigh.

"We all do. They were good people." With a pensive smile he

turned to Kathy. "They were in Tower One of the World Trade Center bombing."

"Oh, no! I'm so sorry, Mitch."

"Thank you."

Dave cleared his throat, "Remember when we tried to teach your mother how to snow ski?"

Simone looked at her husband and pleaded, "Oh, Mitch, tell me you didn't do to her what you did to me!"

With the light restored in his eyes, Mitch replied, "No, we started her off on the bunny hill and she fell every five feet until she got to the bottom."

George and Jake's laughter rang through the restaurant. "Dad and I stayed at the lodge. Warm and toasty," Jake reminded them.

"I told her not to trust those boys," Renee said to Kathy and Simone. "I'm surprised they took it seriously and didn't leave the poor girl at the top of the mountain."

"You'd've skinned us alive, Ma."

"Yes, I would have."

"Besides it was a hell of a lot of fun watching my mom fall and listening to her swear," Mitch informed Renee.

"Something she didn't do often," Dave added with a salute of his drink.

"Jake, you never did anything wild and crazy?" Kathy inquired with her chin resting in her hand.

"Not like these two."

"Jake was too busy being a Boy Scout, Muffin." Dave liked seeing the way her eyes warmed when he called her that—like a sweet little nickname let her know she had his full attention even in a room full of people. "Here, let me hold her." Dave took Emma in his arms when Simone took her out of her highchair.

His leg instinctively started to bounce when he sat the cherub down on his lap.

"I've seen pictures of Jake in that Boy Scout uniform," Sophie announced. "Gosh, you were a looker even then." She leaned into him and Jake kissed her gently on the lips.

"Bet that fine ass I was. But Mitch is leaving out the fact that he'd been a Scout, too."

"Sure was." Simone wrapped an arm through her husband's and leaned into him.

"Really?" Kathy's eyes fell on Mitch, who'd been studying her with curiosity. "What?" she asked.

"You must have some crazy stories, too. Come on, Kathy, we've been hogging the conversation all night."

"Some new stories would be nice," George told her.

"Come on," Dave prompted. When she looked at him and her eyes fell on the baby remorse and yearning filled them.

"Well…I used to sneak Sophie out of her bedroom window to go to late night movies. Did your parents ever find out about that?"

"My dad did. But he never told my mother." Sophie took a sip of her water then retorted, "Kathy's parents are hippies."

"What?" the group queried in unison.

"Thanks, Sophie."

"That's what friends are for."

"What do you mean?" Renee added, leaning forward.

"Genuine hippies. My parents went with their parents to Woodstock. We lived out of a trailer for the first six years of my life and then only tents in the summer. It was awful."

"Wow. I wouldn't have thought that. You seem so…" Dave's words trailed off.

"Conservative?" she answered for him.

"Yeah." He looked down at Emma and kissed her fuzzy head.

She was such a good baby. He hadn't heard her once cry or fuss. Mitch and Simone were truly lucky people.

"Well, you either embrace the life or go the opposite way of it." Kathy lifted the dinner napkin off her lap and began to pick at the fabric.

"She even changed her name," Sophie announced.

"Oh, God. Really? You had to bring that up?"

"Now I see why my boy's so fascinated with you. There's a lot to know. Tell us more," George urged.

"There really isn't any more." Kathy cringed.

In a friendly gesture, Mitch took her hand. "What was your birth name?"

"Aaagggg. Karma Moonshine." At the burst of laughter, Kathy covered her face. "I know. I know. That's why I changed it."

"So," Dave said while handing the baby back to Simone. "Guess I'm not the only one with a crazy history. When did you stop being Karma?"

Pressing her lips together, Kathy looked to Sophie for an out and when she didn't get one she replied, "Sophie brought me. I did it when I was nineteen. I figured no one would take me seriously with a name like that."

Dave took a sip of his beer while eyeing Kathy. "Humph."

Mitch, who still held her hand, asked, "Brothers? Sisters?"

She took a deep breath. "I have one brother, Zen, who's eleven months younger than me."

"Kathy comes from a very eccentric family," Sophie stated.

"That's a sweet way to put it, Soph. My parents and their friends are nudists—on top of being tree huggers."

Dave nearly choked on his beer as he looked at her with wide eyes. "Nudists. As in no clothes?"

"Not a stitch to sleep, swim, or make breakfast in. It wasn't easy growing up…and kinda creepy. Sleepovers were out of the question because my friends' parents didn't want their children subjected to our way of life. Can't really blame them. On top of that, my 'family,' or our colony of naked hippies, thought I was weird because I wore a bathing suit and pajamas by the time I was nine. I refused to see anyone in the buff or them see me. I pretty much isolated myself."

"I can't imagine," Simone announced with disgust.

"It was terrible. My parents' friends would come and hug you and stuff." Kathy acknowledged the horror of it with a fake gag noise.

Dave leaned in and kissed her cheek as his heart ached for the little girl she used to be. "How did they feel about you being different?"

"It's their way of life along with their friends and my grandparents. I don't tell them it's wrong, so they don't tell me mine is."

"George dear, can you imagine us skinny-dipping with youngsters at our age?"

"Absolutely not. I wouldn't want to subject anyone to this body but my lovely wife."

"Thank you, Dad, we appreciate that. Right, Jake?" Dave slapped his brother on the shoulder.

"More than you can possibly understand."

"There is very little in this world that can shock me. Well…at least in the unconservative way." Kathy gave Dave a rueful smile. "Though your tattoos did surprise me."

He leaned into her—wanting to be close and smell her perfume. "I do my best to look the part of outstanding citizen."

"You do it well."

Was she flirting with him in front of his parents? Dave felt pride in knowing she was comfortable enough to let down her guard. He watched his parents, a couple for over thirty years, joke with and kiss each other with unwavering love. Did Kathy's parents love their children and each other like that? Glancing at her and having their eyes meet and hold, Dave's life path suddenly became clear—he was supposed to be in this very spot, at this very moment. Everything he'd been through and had worked toward led up to the realization that loving Kathy was his reward.

When Dave winked at her, heat rose to her ears.

"Why do you do that to me?" she whispered in his ear. "It's so unfair. You know how easy I blush."

"Oh, I haven't made you blush yet," Dave teased.

"Let's not go there, bro," Jake warned, loud and robust.

Sophie leaned over to her man. "Oh, I don't know. I think it's cute. Puppy love. Remember when we talked all mushy to each other."

"I distinctly remember us yelling at each other and—"

"—you running away from me?"

"I never ran from anything."

Dave snorted. "Right. Mitch, what do you think?"

"I remember him running to get your parents when we set the woods on fire....By accident," he assured Kathy.

"I'm sure," Simone retorted.

A dessert of chocolate mousse and strawberries was brought in and everyone gave Sophie an odd look when she refused.

"Are you feeling okay?" Kathy asked her friend, whose hand was resting on her stomach.

"Just the flu. Figures that I'd make it through the winter but not the spring without being sick."

"Are you sure, dear?" Renee leaned over and placed her hand on Sophie's forehead. "You're not pregnant, are you?"

Ghost white and with his mouth gapping open, Jake looked at Sophie with horror. "What? No. Absolutely not."

"Thanks, honey, glad to know you'd be supportive."

"That's not what I meant."

"I know what you meant." Mild irritation oozed from Sophie's words. "I'm sure I'm not expecting any surprises. The doctor said it's a case of the flu and some low iron."

"That's what happened to me when I was first pregnant." Terror streaked across Jake's face when he looked at Simone. "I'm just saying," she told him.

"Well, that's too bad," George said. "We've been waiting for grandchildren for a while now and only Mitch has had the decency to procreate."

"And then we don't get to see him but once every couple years," Renee finished.

"I'm not going to be rushed into anything." Jake defended himself.

"Who said anything about you?" Renee joked. "If the girl's pregnant and you don't like it, then get the hell out."

"Yeah," George agreed. "We like her better, anyway."

"Obviously," Jake grumbled.

"And how about you, Kathy?"

"Dad," Dave warned.

"What? I just want to know how she's feelin' about kids."

The truth was Dave did too, especially with the way she'd been looking at Emma.

Wouldn't they make some nice-looking babies together?

* * *

"I like them," Kathy admitted while smiling at Emma. "And I think having a few would be a ton of fun—and trouble."

"You're not kidding," Renee agreed. "Our David took on all

the trouble our neighbors kids, his cousins, and all his friends would have been in. Bless him for taking that challenge on in the name of fun." She smiled at her son with such love Kathy's eyes began to sting with tears. How she wished her parents looked at her like that.

"Thanks, Ma."

"You did good, boy," George told his son. "Not many people can come back from the dead."

"The dead?" Kathy asked.

The table became very quiet. Mitch shifted in his seat, Sophie excused herself to go the ladies' room with Simone, who needed to change the baby, and Jake grabbed his, his father's, and Mitch's glasses then headed to the bar for refills. Kathy wasn't sure what would be coming next but it felt serious by the thick, nervous air swirling around them.

Renee spoke first as Dave continued to stare at his father with scorn. "Dave had an accident and left us for a short time."

With concern Kathy laid a hand on Dave's shoulder. "What kind of accident?" The shock of his answer rendered her speechless for what seemed to be an eternity but in reality was a half a second.

"It was an overdose on drugs and I spent some time in a coma," he explained.

Dave's eyes bore into hers, daring Kathy to walk. But she wasn't that kind of person. Trust was as important to her as it was to Dave and he needed to know that.

"Dave, my parents are hippies. You think I haven't been around that kind of stuff. Seen something like that happen before? Don't be mad at your father."

"I'm more embarrassed than pissed. I wasn't a drug addict, Kathy."

"I will back you up there, Dave," Mitch assured his friend. "He just got his hands on stuff that was laced with something else."

"Scary," Renee added, then downed the rest of her martini.

"I'm sure. I was twelve when I got my first marijuana contact high. My parents thought it was hilarious. My father's best friend said I was officially a grown-up."

Mitch winced. "Creepy. Your parents didn't protect you much."

"No…they didn't." She felt her eyes blink rapidly while her mind scrambled to find something else to say.

"If I'd listened to my parents, it wouldn't have happened." The disdain with himself was evident, and so was the love all the people at the table had for him.

"Hey, big brother, don't be so hard on yourself." Jake gave Dave a good slap on the back after passing the fresh drinks out to everyone. "My brother here was a real good dancer at one time, too."

Dave buried his head in his hands. "I'm in hell."

"Really?" Kathy's imagination took flight as the thought of Dave stripping down to nothing became an alluring image.

"No!" Dave insisted. "I worked at a strip club not—"

"Oh yes!" Renee confirmed. "Our David can really—"

"Pleasssse, Ma. I've been embarrassed enough tonight." His eyes pleaded with his mother who then reached across the table and gave his face a couple good-natured taps.

"I don't know, Dave, maybe you haven't." Kathy turned to his mother. "What kind of dancing?" she asked with a wink.

George looked uncomfortable. "Can we find something else to talk about?"

"Thank you, Dad."

"You're welcome, Dave. And I'm very happy you don't sell

your body for money anymore." There was a slight twitch to the sides of George's mouth as he struggled to keep a straight face.

"Really?" Dave asked his father. "You're going to throw me to the wolves and let them eat me alive? Kathy, I never stripped in my life! These guys are trying to make me sound like a whore." Even with his dander up Dave still held a sparkle in his eyes for the fun his family was having at his expense.

She pressed her lips together to keep from laughing. If only her own family was as much fun.

"Oh, no, no. I'd never say or think that, son," George assured Dave.

"You pretty much just did!"

"What your father was trying to say," Mitch proclaimed, "is while the job was lucrative—"

Pointing a firm finger at his friend, Dave laughed, "Out of everyone, I thought *you'd* at least stick up for me."

"Nope. I'll throw you under the bus at every possible moment, too."

"He's thrown me plenty of times," Simone interjected.

"So you were never a stripper?" Kathy jested.

"They like to tease but no, I never was," he told her with a smile. "Although I could attempt to give you a striptease if you want?"

Her breath hitched. "I would love that."

* * *

Gosh, she's cute. Dave couldn't help reaching for her thigh under the table and couldn't wait to get his hands on the rest of her. "Tonight? You, me, and that sexy body of yours?"

"Dave." Her evident deep breath said her mind was searching

for a good retort. "Game on. But if you're going to dance for me, it might be useful to use Sophie's dance studio" She smiled seductively. "She has a lot of barres and poles in there."

Rich laughter escaped from everyone at the table. "That'll work."

"How many dollars should I bring?" she asked.

"Not too many. It'll be my first time."

"Modesty will get you nowhere," Renee informed her son. "Mitch dear, when do all of you have to go home?"

"We'll be heading out late tomorrow."

"Mitch and I would really love it if the both of you came to visit us soon," Simone invited.

"We'd love to." George leaned over and kissed his wife. "You have our only grandchild."

Bending down Mitch searched the diaper bag for a bottle. "Kathy, you and Dave, Jake and Sophie should think about coming up too."

Simone gazed down with love at the baby swaddled in her arms. "We have plenty of room and New York City isn't as scary as you'd think."

"That's very nice of you, Mitch."

"Don't let him fool you, Kathy," Dave whispered not so quietly in her ear. "He has ulterior motives."

"He's right. I need someone strong who can help me bring our new deck furniture up ten flights," Mitch confirmed while handing Simone the baby bottle.

Jake clucked his tongue. "Always was a cheap bastard."

"Frugal, Jake. I'm not going to pay hundreds more for someone to do it when I have perfectly capable hands and friends. Plus we really want you guys to come for a visit."

The group of them continued on this way for hours until Jake and Sophie readied to leave Mitch and Simone's hotel room, where they ended up after dinner. They had decided it would be easier if everyone went there in case the baby needed to be put to bed. George and Renee had opted out with the excuse they were still jet-lagged from the flight up but everyone could tell the older couple just wanted to give the old friends time to reconnect.

"Can you believe he's sissying out on us?" Mitch asked Dave.

Both men watched as the huge man squatted down to hug each of the ladies and then give Emma a noisy kiss on her head. He then looked their way. "Later, girls," Jake announced with a salute.

"Later," they replied in unison.

Dave smiled at Kathy from across the room. She was on the floor crawling with Emma.

"I know it's none of my business. But how much did you know about Kathy before tonight?" Mitch asked.

"Apparently not much. She's been a little resistant." Dave frowned.

"Haven't you two been dating?"

Dave gave a laugh that ended with a snort. "No, not really. You kinda showed up at the beginning of my wooing."

"Wooing? Ha! You've never persuaded any woman in your life." But Mitch leaned toward him with serious eyes. "I like her. I really do, Dave."

"But?"

"I think there's more there. I don't know. Maybe I'm talking out my ass." Mitch pondered and took a long sip of his beer.

"You don't think she's marriage material?"

"That's not what I'm saying."

"Then what are you saying? Because I'm damn close to being in love with her and feeling a little—"

"Defensive?" Mitch asked with a chuckle.

"Yeah."

Mitch took an uneasy breath and said what was on his mind. "I think you need to know her better before making grand plans in that thick skull of yours."

"Didn't you know right away when you saw Simone? What's so different about this?"

Both men turned and looked at the women in their lives. Simone was currently tickling the baby's feet and Kathy was laughing.

"Yeah, I did know," Mitch began. "It was like a cement truck running me over. This is different though."

Dave pressed his lips together and rolled his eyes to the ceiling. "Why can't everyone just be happy for me? There's always strings attached, someone trying to cut me off at the knees."

"That's not what I'm doing. And I'm totally screwing this up. Look, Dave—"

"No, you look." Dave poked a finger in Mitch's chest. "I have a damn cop on my ass and a business that's barely holding on because of the recession. My parents are worried I'm getting depressed, not to mention pressuring me to settle down. Then my dad looks like hell and I'm wondering if he's having heart problems again but doesn't want to worry anyone," Dave said. "Not to mention, I need to get a new car but haven't really done much planning for that financially so it's been pushed to the back burner for now." Dave pulled an agitated hand through his hair.

"Don't you have anything in savings, Dave?" Mitch asked.

"Yeah, but every time I get behind the wheel my heart starts racing. Jake gets it but it annoys the shit out of me."

"Gotcha. You need time, Dave. No one's going to blame you for that. At least you have someone there for you. I'm not sure Kathy does."

Dave looked long and hard at his friend then over at the woman he was referring to. "What do you mean?"

"Firs, do you feel better after getting that off your chest?"

"Ha, ha. Yeah."

"Personally, I think you should take it slower with Kathy."

Dave sat back in his chair then started rotating the beer bottle around. "Why do you think so?"

"Maybe it's that girly sensitive side of me—"

"Always had us wondering what team you were playing for," Dave said with a smirk.

"Whatever. But that girl's been hurt…bad."

"Ex-husband." Dave retorted without thought. "Bad sexual partners."

"Right. But I'm thinking it's deeper than that. Family stuff."

Dave's eyes met Mitch's serious ones. "Maybe I'm getting dense. Are you saying you think…yuck…that it's her family. You think they're that open with each other?"

Mitch's mild look of annoyance had Dave pressing his lips together. "You are thick, Dave. You know that, right? No. I don't think they had sex with each other, I think maybe something happened with one of her parents' friends. Geez."

Mulling this over for a minute Dave opened his mouth to say, "No way!" but nothing came out. Instead he took another sip of beer and ate a handful of popcorn. It would explain so much. Kathy had said he couldn't shock her father. That he'd have to meet him to understand. The picture of her childhood and the distrust she had in herself and others began to get clearer. "I don't want to think about that. Maybe you're right but maybe you're not."

"All I'm saying is listen a little harder to what she says. I think she's more scared than shy."

"Gives a lot of mixed signals, too."

"It would explain why," Mitch added.

Dave pondered his friend's family with a ping of envy. "You have a nice family, Mitch. Someday I really hope to have my own."

"You will."

It was well after two in the morning before Dave slid into bed. His parents were sleeping down the hall in the room they'd occupied since he and Jake had been children. After he bought the home from them, Dave couldn't bring himself to move into the bigger bedroom. That would remain his parents' room, no matter how many changes he made to the place. New kitchen with oak cabinets, heated tile floor, top-of-the-line appliances, and walls knocked down to open up the whole first floor. The only thing not new was the casing around the back door where his parents measured him and Jake every first day of school. There was a bathroom added to a finished cellar. And his pride always burst at the seams when people asked about the wraparound porch he built onto the two-story cape. Jake said it would look odd but after adding a new wood front door with side windows and bigger living room windows with new siding, the exterior looked and felt original. Dave made the home into the place he wanted to raise his children and live out his days married to the woman of his dreams.

But as comfortable as his bed was, as much as his body wanted to drift into the land of images and fantasies, Dave's mind wouldn't let him. Instead he thought about Kathy and the traumatic childhood she only hinted at having. If things were as bad as Mitch seemed to think, would she consider a life with him? Dave's stomach churned and twisted. He really hoped so because somehow Kathy had become one of the most important people in his life.

Chapter 11

Looking out her apartment window, Kathy saw the glistening sun warming everything its vibrant fingers could touch. It happened overnight. Spring decided to make its grand entrance. Daffodils' sunny petals smiled. Trees that had been barren with sticklike fragility now had soft buds ready to burst. People were about raking and cleaning up the winter mess on their lawns. *A perfect day.* Maybe she would go for a run or a stroll with Dave.

Lately he seemed to fill her mind more and more. After dinner with his family and Mitch, their relationship changed from casual to intimate. The potent attraction was now something deeper, newer, sweeter. A week ago she had asked him to be patient and Dave did back off without any questions. However he now called or texted her every morning when he woke—just to say "Hi" and Kathy couldn't have been happier. On one occasion, after discovering she loved Greek food, he surprised her with a cozy dinner for two with candles and soft music on his living room floor. They kissed passionately then he laid her back on the floor and covered her body with his. She held him tightly against her as she opened her legs so he'd fit more comfortably between them. Dave was rigid everywhere; his back, his bottom, his arms. And when his firm lips traveled to her earlobe and nipped, she wished his parents weren't in the other room. Kathy wondered, on more than one occasion, if maybe they weren't ever going to be together in that special way. Wanting him to touch her, hold her, and lie naked next to each other was becoming almost an obsession—a fantasy she needed to have fulfilled. The powerful want Dave created in her pushed Todd, and the moments his memories had marred with other men, away. With Dave there would be only them in that intimate embrace, no ghost of her ex and their past standing over them.

Dave believed in the little things, which only swelled her heart more with what felt precariously close to love. Every day he would bring her coffee to work with a hot cinnamon bun. Then, for no reason at all, he began picking her up so they could drive in together. He still had Jake's car, and didn't seem to be in a hurry to get one of his own.

With him on her mind, Kathy got in the shower. What surprise would he have for her today? There was always something. The weekend before Dave convinced her to go over to his place for a barbecue. Then he cornered Kathy with questions on the type of flowers she thought he should plant around his home. She was surprised by how much he genuinely cared for her opinion.

"I'm sick of the grass going right up to the foundation. It looks so bland," he told her.

"I agree." Kathy scratched her head. "I'm really not that good with stuff like this. I never had a garden." She laughed. "Or anything close to a yard of my own."

On a laugh he kissed her cheek. "Here's the chance. We can figure it out together."

"I don't know." She bit her lower lip and squinted at the front of his cape home. "Maybe you should call a landscaper."

"Er. Little expensive for me."

"Well, do you want a lot of flowers or shrubs?"

"I guess shrubs. But then I'd have to trim all the time, right?"

Kathy sat on the front steps. "I hadn't thought of that. Umm, I guess you should go with the flowers then."

"What kind of flowers?"

"The ones that come back and the ones that you have to keep planting," she told him.

"Not sure. Die and thrive—maybe?" She giggled at Dave's response. "Muffin, you're damn near irresistible when you do that." Placing his hands on her knees, he leaned down and gave her a kiss that seemed to touch her soul.

"Dave, stop that. Your neighbors could be watching. And you're making me want to rip your clothes off and take you right here."

"I don't mind. That might be kinda fun." He sat down next to her.

Ultimately Dave was able to convince her to help the very next day and the following weekends. Heck, it sounded as if she'd be there for the whole yard transformation. Thinking about it now, a light came on in Kathy's head. It seemed awfully convenient, and a total ploy, that he needed help when she knew he was good with plants because the inside of his house was full of them. She made a face at herself in the mirror. She couldn't deny the excitement running through her at the thought of spending more time with him.

The phone rang and she ran to answer it with enthusiasm. "Morning!"

"Hi, Kathy."

Her world went still.

"What do you want, Todd? I thought I made myself clear that I don't want to talk to you."

"I—"

"What?" She demanded.

"I don't like the way we left things. And I didn't get a chance to tell you I'm happy to hear you found a job. It's very tough in this economy to be laid off and then find work."

"So."

"I think it's super."

"Thanks," she replied with a desert-dry tone.

Todd cleared his throat. "I've been thinking—"

"Wow, that's new." It really wasn't. Kathy had heard him use that opening line often to get people to do things for him. "Must not be doing too much of it 'cause I thought I made myself clear last time we saw each other."

"Kathy, I miss you and I'm so sorry for the times I caused you pain. But I'm a different person now."

"I'm sure."

"No. I really am." His plea fell on deaf ears and when she didn't respond to his declaration, Todd continued. "I know it's been a long time. Hell, years. But I still think about you and wonder what's going on. Losing you broke my heart and now, with..." he trailed off obviously wanting her to think about him dying.

"Good-bye, Todd."

Kathy slammed the phone down and when it rang two seconds later, fury engulfed her. "What! I don't want to talk to you. Stop calling!"

This time when she hit the end button, she also unplugged the phone from the wall. At the burst of unexpected tears, Kathy sank to the floor. The treason of what her parents did hit her hard. How could they not stick up for her? Didn't they want what was best for their daughter? Throughout their relationship all Todd did was lie, be selfish, break promises, and hurt her. He said he would get a job, and that the whole financial burden would not be on her. But in the end every job he got turned into one he lost or quit. No one treated him right; he was looked down upon; they didn't appreciate his work and all he did for them. And her favorite excuse, "I don't think working is for me. I'm still trying to find myself." Oh yes, Todd always seemed to be "finding" himself. The stinker was that her parents "understood" him and thought she should be more sympathetic. After all they once needed to do the same thing. But Kathy was eighteen for goodness sakes! She wasn't supposed to be taking care of anyone, they should have been doing that for her. Her parents said he was the best thing to ever happen to her. That they were so proud of her. Now he was supposedly dying. What kind of person was she to turn away a terminally ill man?

No, she wasn't going to do this. Todd was the past and he would stay there forever. He was never there for her emotionally—only her for him. He couldn't understand why she didn't want to live like traveling gypsies and why it was so important to her to have a job with welcomed responsibilities. But Dave did. He was a stand-up kind of guy who knew both sides of this sometimes awful world. And he appreciated her, liked all her quirks, and never asked her to do anything she didn't feel comfortable with. Why would she leave such a wonderful man to go back to that lowlife loser and her parents?

Wiping the tears from her face and pulling up her imaginary big girl panties, Kathy did an emotional moving on. *Sometimes,* she told herself, *the only way to get to where you want to be, is to be the strongest person you know.*

She stood straight and rolled her shoulders back. This was the ending of an era. From here on out she was going to be her own person. Looking out the window at the cloudless sky she did a mental midday sunset on the past and all its afflictions. No more. She was going to break all her bad habits until there was nothing left but the positive of a new day.

The powerless phone mocked her resolve but didn't weaken it. She would plug it back in. And when he called back Kathy would inform him that there would be a restraining order issued if he didn't stop.

Feeling a sense of relief Kathy did just that. No more running, no more being the victim; even if she never thought of herself that way, sometimes she knew she acted like one.

The cell phone in her purse began to ring—the vibration causing the small bag to dance on her counter. "Hello?"

"Kathy?"

"Oh, hi, Dave. What's up?" Relief washed over her voice with hearing his.

"Everything all right, Muffin? I tried the house phone but—"

"Sorry about that. I unplugged it."

"Yeahhhh. Umm. That was me on the other line."

Kathy's mind blanked. "Oops."

Dave's laughter sang through the phone. "Oops? I thought you were talking to me. Everything okay?"

She gave a heavy sigh. "Yeah."

"Really? There's nothing you want to share? Or do you randomly yell at people on the phone? Because if that's what you do, let me know. We could always use it as a form of foreplay." With a devilish laugh, he added, "Then have makeup sex."

"Is your head always in the gutter, Mr. Sanders?"

"Absolutely."

"At least you're honest. My ex-husband called."

"Why?"

"Who knows? My parents gave him my number."

"Why the hell would your parents give him your number?"

Kathy sat with a helpless plop on her sofa. "Who knows? I never know why they do the things they do." She inhaled a deep breath and prepared herself to tell Dave the whole truth about her ex. "As for Todd, he's trying to get back together with me. Apparently he's dying and wants to make amends before he goes to the fiery depths. Personally I think he needs money for his medical expenses."

There was a small growl on the other end of the line. "Have you ever given him money?"

"No! And I don't care what his pathetic story is. He won't get it and I want nothing to do with him."

"Thank God because I'm not about to give you up!"

She needed to be honest with Dave and herself and wanted him to know exactly what her heart was telling her. "I couldn't give you up, either."

There was silence for a moment and then, "Kathy, you mean a lot to me and I think you should be careful. He seems like trouble."

"He's harmless."

"I don't like it, Kathy."

The dryness in Dave's voice brought a smile to her lips. "Interesting. Are you jealous, Dave?"

"Maybe." He laughed. "Does it turn you on?"

"Maybe." She licked her lips and wished he was there so she could do naughty things to him.

"We're going out to eat tonight at the Blue Room. Seven o'clock. Wear something sexy with very little underneath it."

"Mmm…very provocative. Any particular color, Mr. Sanders?"

"I love you in all colors."

His low throaty response sent a breathtaking shiver through her body. "And what do you have planned for after this very expensive dinner?" She couldn't wait to hear his response and bit her lower lip in the anticipation of it—the small amount of pain bringing her pleasure.

"You're going to have to use your imagination."

An intense heat traveled through her at the excitement of what was to come. "I'm going to need to buy a dress."

"I can't wait to see it."

She swallowed hard. Was she going to be able to handle this man? "Dave?"

"Don't be nervous, Muffin. It's just me and you. And if you ever want me to stop, I will."

"Okay."

But she was as worried as a virgin on prom night anticipating becoming a woman. Even after Sophie's help with picking out a backless deep red dress an hour later, Kathy began questioning what she was doing. She shaved everything that could possibly be, without going overboard. Then she moisturized her whole body with vanilla-scented lotion.

Anxious and jumpy she leaned over to pull up a thigh-high, lost her balance and, on a scream, went headfirst into the edge of her dresser. In a bra, panties, and with half a stocking on, her cheek sang. She sat where she landed with a hand to the already swelling area and laughed like a loon. This could only happen to her. She was just glad she didn't kill herself. The morning paper would read: *Woman Killed in Hosiery Accident*. Aagggg!

Disorientated Kathy staggered to the kitchen and bumped into every wall along the way. Half a stocking dragged behind her because she feared bending over to pull it all the way up would make her head pulse more than it already was. She grabbed an ice pack from the freezer in hopes it would be her savior and stop the redness. About to go back to her room to finish dressing, she did an about-face, downed some pain pills, and found a mirror.

"The excuse 'I've got a headache' isn't going to be used tonight," she told herself.

Examining her cheek a little closer she began to laugh again. "Great. Now I'm going to look like my date beat me. So much for a romantic night of endless passion." Touching the swollen area with gentle fingers she wondered if Dave would take one look at her and cancel. "Well, not if I have anything to say about it."

Now more determined than ever, Kathy dressed the part of sex kitten. She did her best putting on makeup while holding the ice pack to her cheek. Considering she only poked herself in the eye twice, the ordeal was considered a success.

"Not bad," she told herself in the mirror. Single-eyed, she managed to make sure her lips were the focal point of her face and not the darkening circle around her eye that she tried to cover up with concealer. Next she curled her hair into soft waves. After slipping on the five-inch black strappy heels, Kathy did a turn in front of the dressing mirror. She felt a little giddy, sexy, and ready to take Mr. Sanders on.

After cocking her head for a better examination in the mirror, a dizzying sensation bogged down her mind. With careful steps she sat on her bed just as the doorbell rang. A sigh of resolve passed her lips. "Time to face the music, Kathy. Or his utter shock when he sees what you did to yourself."

By the clock on the wall Kathy realized Dave had come a half an hour early. Good thing she finished getting ready. Being late and ill-prepared always put her in a bad mood. But when she opened the door, it wasn't Dave who stood there. Instead it was Detective Owen.

"Well this day just keeps getting better," Kathy mumbled.

"I'm sorry to disturb you, Miss Smith, especially since you look like you're headed out for the evening."

"What can I do for you, detective?"

"I was wondering if we could go over the report you filed about the bar fight."

"Now is not a good time."

"It'll only take a minute. I want to tie up some loose ends."

Owen's eerie eyes first gazed at her legs then leisurely drew up to her breasts and then her face. Kathy did all she could to not shiver and cover herself up. The man made her feel dirty.

"No," she replied firmly. "If you need me to do that then you should have called and asked me to come to the station. I don't appreciate you coming to my home." Kathy raised her chin and attempted to close the door in his face when Owen slapped a palm on it.

"I'm only asking for a minute of your time."

With a look of annoyance, she glared at Owen's chubby hand. "I'm sorry but I'm on my way out. I'll be down first thing Monday. Can I help you with anything else?"

His hand dropped while his eyes narrowed. "I underestimated you, Miss Moonshine."

"Miss Smith. You say my former name like it's some dark secret." She waved her hands in the air. "Oooo."

Owen's lips twitched, then with a nod of his head he turned his back to her and walked away. "Have a good time tonight, Karma. Hope that black eye won't put a damper on it."

She slammed the door then spied out the peephole. He was gone. On a sigh, Kathy went to the kitchen to make a cup of tea to calm her nerves. Damn him for getting her upset before her date with Dave! Wasn't she already nervous enough?

Just to make sure the bruising wasn't as bad as Owen made it out to be, Kathy went to the bathroom to examine herself in the mirror.

"Really? You had to be this clumsy today? Out of all the days?" The dark bloom on her cheek had expanded up the side of her face and now mixed with her eye makeup. She would either have to touch up the other eye and risk looking like a prostitute, or leave it alone and let the world know that she practically knocked her own butt out.

The kettle whistled loud and the screeching knocked around in Kathy's head as she moved back into the kitchen. The rhythmic beat of her clicking heels echoed off the empty walls in her apartment. Growing up the way she did, Kathy always had very little and spending time in Dave's home had her realizing how empty her apartment really was.

Opening a cabinet, she took down one of her four coffee cups to finish making her green tea. Leaving it to steep she took a survey of her barren place. White walls, no artful throw rugs placed or hung photos to make the place cozy. The only plant, which Sophie bought her after the divorce years earlier, sat on the tiny kitchen table that boasted two chairs. The one thing that made her home look lived in was the coffee machine sitting on the Formica counter. It was all very depressing. *This isn't a home. It's a place to rest your head.* She had no emotional attachment to it, no pull to be there when the day was too rough for words. It was all very sad, very lonely.

She sipped her tea and tried to talk herself into buying some curtains. Maybe something with bold colors and a crazy print. But Kathy couldn't quite summon up any excitement over the prospect and decided she must really not want them, so why bother?

At the rap on the door a slow smile formed on her lips. *Dave.* It had to be him. If there was anyone else at that door, she would flip out.

Chapter 12

Dave couldn't believe his clumsiness. First he cut his chin shaving, then he stubbed his toe on the corner of his bedroom door, which left him with a small limp. In the middle of it all, his parents announced they were staying another week. After some hemming and hawing Dave finally told them, without coming out directly and saying it, what he planned for the evening with Kathy. He then, not so politely, told them to get the hell out and stay at Jake's. At least they didn't put up a fight about it.

He adjusted the pants waist of his suit with one hand while he clutched the yellow daisies with the other. Maybe he shouldn't have bought them, they were so cliché and he always strived not to be. *But this is Kathy,* he reminded himself. Nervousness and second guessing were getting the best of him. What had come over him from this morning? He had been so confident, so ready for this.

The sensation to turn and run was about to win over his eagerness to see her when the door opened. There she stood with tall heels, miles of leg, and—she turned during his survey—backless. The dress seemed to be completely nonexistent. She peered over her left shoulder at him and smiled.

"Dear Lord. Please don't let me be dreaming. Tell me you're real." He swallowed hard to remove the lump in the back of his throat.

"I'm very real, Mr. Sanders. Do you want to come in?"

She grinned at him over her shoulder until, unable to control himself any longer, he grabbed her arm, spun her around, and pressed his mouth to hers. He wanted her to feel his frenzy; to need what he needed; be the only thing on her mind as she was for him.

Crushing her body to his, Dave moved them into the apartment and kicked the door shut. "Let's just stay here," he said, moving his lips to her ear.

"No way. You got me dressed up, you're taking me out." She leaned into him, "God, you always smell so good!"

He had planned to take her to dinner then spend a nice evening at his home; however, with her in his arms, nothing else seemed to matter.

"Okay, but we're eating fast. And—what the hell happened?" He held her face in his hands. The mere idea that her skin had been marred, that someone might have done this to her, threw Dave into a mix of emotions he could barely control. He could taste the blood he desperately wanted from whatever or whoever did this to her. With hands that weren't as gentle as he would have liked, Dave cupped Kathy's face in them.

"It's not that bad."

"Muffin, you have a black eye. Have you put ice on it?" At her look of annoyance he said, "Don't roll your eyes at me. I want to know what happened."

She pulled away from him with a snap. "I'm a klutz, okay?"

"No, it's not okay. Tell me what's going on?" Dave led her to sit on the small, hard as brick couch. "Comfy," he said offhandedly.

"I don't come in here much."

Dave surveyed the unadorned walls and barren windows. The room, much like what he'd seen in the entryway, looked sterile and unloved. A complete contrast to her office, which boasted adventurous pictures of her and Sophie, a few plants, and a candy jar full of trail mix. He always stole all the M&Ms but Kathy didn't seem to mind. "Aren't you afraid someone could be watching you?"

"I have the shades."

Looking from the measly surroundings and to the woman next to him, Dave couldn't help the chuckle that rose in his throat. "Your office has more decoration. Last time I was here the lights weren't on."

"No, they weren't. Wish it was dark now, too."

Dave took her hand in his. "I don't. You look beautiful. Now how'd you get the shiner?"

"It's really very embarrassing. Can we forget about it?"

"No."

"At least until later? No one attacked me or anything. It was just stupid."

How could he say "no" to her with those big brown eyes pleading? He was a goner. Sunk. Drowned. No life vest could save him. "Damn it. Okay. But you won't get out of this again."

Kathy glanced down at the crushed flowers sitting next to Dave. "Those for me?"

"Maybe."

"Well if they're not you better find yourself another date for tonight."

He loved when she teased. The fact that she seemed to be doing it more often made him want to pull it out of her as much as he could. "What if I said they're for a woman who I've dreamed about since the day we met? That I didn't believe in love at first sight until I saw her across the room."

"I'd say you're an incredible romantic and full of shit."

Dave shook his head while laughing. He told her the truth about his past and she accepted it—was even turned on by it. Then he comes clean about his feelings and she can't trust it. "You're the most incredibly confusing woman."

He kissed her then, sweetly. All smoldering passion with the promise of love. How could he convince her that she belonged in his arms? Didn't she feel it, too? His heart felt the need to explode from the love, fright, and pain she caused him. Yet he didn't want the sensation to go away. It felt more like freedom than prison. Unexpected tears burned his eyes. *What the hell is that?* Never the crier, his mind baffled at the reaction. Pulling her into his arms he took in the sweet scent of her perfumed neck.

"You smell good enough to eat," he told her while trying to give himself time to pull his thoughts together.

"You smell delicious and I can't wait to taste you," she replied.

On impulse Dave stood and held out a hand. "Let's go before I drag you to the bedroom and never get to show you off. Every man and woman is gonna be jealous."

She took a deep breath before placing her hand in his. "I don't know what to say when you talk like that."

"Don't. Just kiss me."

She did. And he felt their souls merge, even if only for a split second. "I'll go grab a vase. Thank you for the flowers."

"Thank you for wearing that dress…Sophie?"

They were both laughing upon entering the kitchen. "Who else? I must have tried on hundreds of them and this one covered the most skin."

"I love it." Dave did a three-sixty turn in the tiny kitchen. "You really aren't much for the decorating, are you?"

Kathy pulled out a chubby green vase with different colored polka dots. The whimsical item gave Dave a glance at the side she never seemed to want to people to know about.

"What's the point? Sooner or later I'll move and have to drag everything with me."

She was filling the vase with water then placing it on the kitchen table next to her only plant when Dave realized how Kathy's home was a showcase for her insecurities. If she spent the time and grew attached to where she was living, it would break her heart if she moved. Interesting because it also seemed to be the way she dealt with her relationships. *But not this one,* Dave promised, *she and I are going to paint the walls and then cover them with memories.*

Kathy turned to him and smiled. "I really love the flowers, thank you."

"You're very welcome…again." He did a little bow and a giggle. "Is my lady ready to eat?"

Taking his offered hand, Kathy replied, "Why yes, my lord. I'm famished."

* * *

She tried to think back, wondered if her brain had simply wiped any existence of it: did she ever enjoy a date before this one?

"What?" she asked, while swirling the wine.

"Nothing," Dave said while still smiling at her.

"Now that's just a lie. I'm sure your mother told you lying isn't very nice."

"She's actually boxed my ears a few times because of it."

The slow Italian music sang to them while the candlelight at the table made Dave look more handsome then any man she'd ever set eyes on. Kathy couldn't wait to get her hands on him. They talked so easily and she started to wonder if maybe she was getting a little too obsessed. For cripes sake, she spent most of dinner turned on by the fact he was wearing a suit—and he looked delicious in it.

Shaking her head and clearing the fog, she asked, "Dave?"

"What?"

"You okay? Since we got here you seem really distracted." She reached across the table to him.

"I am." Bringing her hand to his lips, Dave first kissed her palm then, quick as a whip, touched the sensitive spot with his tongue. "I want to pay the bill and bring you home with me."

She rose to her feet as fast as her heels would allow. "I really want that, too."

Actually she wanted him to race that car down the streets, blow all the red lights they hit, and, caution be damned, not care if there were any cops. When they pulled into his drive and came to a sudden halt, both their bodies were pushed forward.

Kathy snickered. "We're nuts."

"Totally," Dave announced while getting out of the car to race around to her side.

When she stepped out of his vehicle, Dave pulled her into his arms and gave her a peck on the lips. "Come on, I have some wine out breathing."

"Really?" She stayed one step behind him as they walked to his door. Taking her by surprise, Dave welcomed Kathy into his home by sweeping her off her feet and walking her over the threshold.

"What would you like to do first?" he asked.

She wrapped her arms tight around his neck while her eyes fell on the many candles that lit up his home. "That's a loaded question." When he only grinned at her, she continued her inspection. "Weren't you afraid those would burn down your home?"

"Yup, that's why I have the battery ones."

After being placed gently on her feet, Kathy walked to one of the lit pillars and picked it up. "Really? That's neat."

"You could use some at your place. Or you could come here and admire mine."

Astonishment engulfed her as she looked from the candles to the floor where different colored petals were laid out like breadcrumbs down the hall and into a bedroom. "I don't know what to say. No one has ever done something like this for me."

"Shame on them." With one finger he pushed the spiky bangs away from her eyes. "I want you to know you're special."

"You make me feel that way." In her heels they were eye to eye. She could see the emotions swirling in his gaze and acknowledged that this moment was about more than candles, flowers, and wine. Dave wanted serious. Was that what she wanted? The answer was a simple "yes." This man always seemed to be thinking of her and endlessly seeking ways to make her day better. Right now his expression told her she was the center of his world—a place she'd never been before with anyone else.

She touched her lips to his and let every passionate sensation he awakened in her out.

Forgetting the wine, Dave once again swept her into his arms. He carried her to his bedroom, a woman's romantic fantasy come true. She'd always dreamt about it. Had even asked Todd to do it once, just so she could live it, but he had a "bad back."

A moment of hesitation swept over her. Butterflies swarmed in her stomach and she tried fruitlessly to calm them. Things were about to change. This step, this moment, embedded a vital element in the rest of their lives.

Dave stood her on her heels and only stared—his surveying eyes taking all of her in. However, instead of feeling self-conscious, she felt liberated and brave. Without touching he leaned into her so they both would lie back on his bed together. Never having felt this kind of connection before, the marvel of experiencing it grew inside her as she felt the urge to bring not only their bodies together as one but also their minds.

Mouths leisurely feasted as Kathy's trembling hands began unbuttoning his shirt. Yet it was not nerves that made her quake but excitement for the pleasures to come. This was what she had been missing. His smell engulfed her, an intoxicating scent of male strength and need. The strong, inked arms quietly massaged her thighs and breasts while he whispered to her.

"You're so beautiful." Dave pulled one of her shoulder straps down with his teeth then moved to the next to do the same.

"I've been waiting for you forever, Dave." Kathy kissed him soundly, hoping he could feel not only her need for him but the emotions that pulled at her to be with him…always.

He straddled her then sat back on his haunches and ran one finger from her ear, down her neck, to the low dip of her cleavage. "Exquisite."

Her mind drew a blank. This man seriously wanted her—all of her.

Leaning up to him, she parted his open shirt to run kisses over his chest. "I love seeing you in a suit and tie." Hearing his sharp intake of breath, Kathy's bravado became stronger. Her hands ran over the taut muscles until they found the snap of his pants. She wanted him all to herself. Craved the desire he stirred inside her, and sought to make him as dazzled as she.

Once the zipper came down she worked his pants lower on his hips until he sprang up, an invitation before her.

"Kathy, there's so much I want to do to you."

"I know." She looked into his crazed eyes and knew he was with her. He would submit to whatever she wanted. "But right now I want to taste you."

Once more she lay back on the bed but this time urged his body to move up as she scooted down. Straddled over her face, he carefully lowered himself into her mouth. With his hands braced on the bedrails above her, Kathy pushed to bring him to the edge of delirium. She worked her hands, tongue, and mouth in a torturous tirade of motion. He moaned, no growled, and pulled himself out only to replace the emptiness with his mouth.

"You win," he told her, as his hands worked her dress off.

Kathy wondered what his reaction would be when he saw the black garter and stockings she wore beneath the silky fabric. She had hoped he would be shocked, maybe even speechless. Her answer came as an outburst of disbelief.

"I'm totally dreaming. There is no way a woman like you would be with a man like me."

"Dave, there's so much inside of me for you."

His head darted between her thighs. Kisses and little nips. Strong hands gripping, then soft caresses. The tangled emotional ball that started to grow inside her the moment he brought her into his bedroom, now grew to an unbearable size. Hot fire— *no that's not right*—blazing pleasure, that's what she felt. When Dave moved her panties aside and covered her with his mouth, her body bowed back and she screamed. Her body had never known such pleasures.

Dave then took his time undoing every snap on the garter

and rolling her stockings down. They locked eyes and she knew he could see the powerful desire she had for him. Kissing her foot, he slowly moved his way up her leg. She leaned back on her elbows enthralled in his journey.

"I love your legs," he told her.

"I think that's all you want from me," she jested.

Dave winked at her then continued his path to her stomach. "Lie back."

"Whatever you want, Mr. Sanders."

On a moan he moved to one of her breasts then the other. "I don't want to leave any part of you out."

Her hands moved through his hair and then pulled his face down so his lips would come back to hers. "You're very thorough, I doubt that'll happen."

Positioning himself between her legs, Dave teased, "Maybe I don't want this part to end so fast." He reared up and then flipped Kathy on her stomach before she could comprehend the change. Then he lay over her while his hands caressed her body beneath him. His hot breath in her ear told erotic tales that only made her more ready for him to end this torment. Her rear end bucked up and he slid his rigid shaft between her cheeks.

"What do you want me to do?"

"You know what I want." Frustrated she worked again to line him up with her vibrating entrance, to slide him in and end the teasing. But each time she tried he out-maneuvered her.

"I don't know unless you tell me," he told her while reaching a hand between her and the mattress to roll a nipple between his fingers.

"Oh, my God! Please, David."

"Please what?"

His hand searched lower to where heat pumped out of her.

When his fingers lightly teased her, she tried to push into them but to no avail. He was in command.

"Tell me."

Her resolve snapped and she felt her mind release all control of her body. "Take me. Make mad passionate love to me. I want to feel you inside me."

He flipped her back over and crushed his mouth to hers. "Tell me again. Right now as I'm entering you."

"I want you, Dave. I need you."

So slow, so agonizing. He didn't seem to move fast enough so she wrapped her legs around his bottom and pushed him in. Bright lights went off behind her closed lids like fireworks. Once inside her he ceased movement. Every nerve seemed to be on high alert. Her muscles quivered with unexpected pleasure. Dave, braced above her, smiled then lowered his lips to hers.

There were no quick jolting moves. He took his time with her and together they became one. Mind, body, and soul.

* * *

It was after two when Dave rolled over to look at the clock. They had managed to drink the wine—even pour a little on each other and then sip it off. He laughed and Kathy joined him.

"What are we laughing about?" she asked.

"I was thinking about the wine. And the strawberries and the whipped cream."

"Let's not forget the Pixy Stix you found."

"Mmmm." He rolled over and onto her. "You're beautiful."

"Really? You can see me in the dark?"

"I can see you in my mind." He rubbed his nose to hers. "How do you feel?"

"Wonderful." Her hands moved up his naked body to rest on his shoulders. "I haven't been this relaxed since...well, I don't know."

"Good. I plan on keeping you this way." He hadn't expected to make the kiss so passionate but now that he developed a taste for her, it sure seemed hard to stop.

"Again?" she asked on a laugh.

"Again." Dave pulled the covers over their heads and had his way with her for a third time.

An hour later he was sated and began to drift off to sleep when he felt the bed move. He opened an eye when Kathy turned on the light. "Where are you going?"

"Home." She told him while collecting her clothes.

"Excuse me?" Dave yawned.

"Home. Everyone knows that men prefer the woman to leave. I don't want to overstay my welcome."

"We've already proven, multiple times, that you've been with the wrong men. I'm not one of them." He held out a hand. "Stay." The contemplation in her face pleased him. This was what she wanted as well but was too afraid. "Stay," he repeated.

Dave never dropped his hand until hers was in his. He stayed awake until he heard the sweet sounds of her slumber. He never knew what love truly was until the moment she turned her body into his and snuggled as close as two people could get.

Chapter 13

Kathy had just gotten out of her car and was reminiscing about the previous night with Dave when she stopped dead in her tracks. Pain streaked through her psyche as apprehension froze her in place. *This can't be happening.* Her parents had showed up in a spray-painted bright pink van. For as long as she lived Kathy would never understand why they did the things they did. Looking around her apartment parking lot she couldn't help but wonder if she should make a run for it. Maybe she was wrong and that wasn't her parents' van? She hadn't seen them yet, right? They hadn't called to say they were coming for a visit if they even owned a phone. Things had ended badly on their last stopover when Evaan and Telia expressed that they needed the phones and expected Kathy to let them use her credit to get them. Not only did they want her to sign the cell plan, they wanted her to give *her* credit card number for payment and they would send her money every month. *Yeah, right.*

Kathy stood in the afternoon sun, the cheery light beams smiling upon her shoulders and the new warmth of spring made the air smell fresh and new. She closed her eyes and hoped when they opened the van would be gone. It wasn't. And as she walked to it Kathy remembered the news report only a few days after her parents left last time. An old trailer in Rector County that was part of a traveling RV group had been seized. Contents: massive amounts of marijuana and drug paraphernalia; people responsible: unknown. Kathy laughed so hard her sides hurt. She knew it had been her parents' place because the news showed the inside of the confiscated RV decorated with wild colors and crazy decor. Anyone who knew Evaan and Telia knew it was them.

Biting the bullet Kathy knocked on the van door and hoped she was wrong. But when it slid open, her father's face split into a grin.

"Karma! Honey, come look! It's Karma."

"Oh, we missed you so much!" Telia leaped out of the bubble gum–colored vehicle and hugged her daughter. "I'd been afraid you moved because you didn't come home last night."

They smelled bad, like they hadn't showered in a week. She cleared her throat before her gag reflex fully developed. "Why don't you come inside and clean up," she offered.

"Do you have any food?" Evaan looked hopeful.

"I'm sure there's something. I have a few hours before work so that'll give you enough time to clean up and do whatever it is you need to do." As Kathy walked away from them, her heart pulled at her to be nicer, while her brain said not to let them stay at her place.

"Can I do some laundry?" her mother called out.

"You have enough time for one load."

Kathy rushed into her residence then kicked off her high heels. They landed with a thump against the entryway wall. At least she had on a jacket to cover the back of her dress. Not that

that would stop them from commenting on her attire. Her feet marched down the hall and into her room where she slammed the door with retaliation. Damn them for coming and ruining her day. Now instead of going to work and giving Dave seductive eyes, talking him into letting her come over for "dinner," she would have to be home making sure nothing got stolen. With her mood ever souring, Kathy began undressing.

"Karma, dear!" her father called out. "Where are you?"

"I'm changing." The doorknob jiggled, reminding Kathy why, even after years of living on her own, she still locked the door when she changed.

"I'd like to talk to you about something serious," Evaan told her.

"I already know about Todd, Dad. And I'll be out in a minute."

"I know you do. We talked to him and—"

"Damn it! I'll be out in a minute!" She sat on the bed with her face in her hands. *Why did they never listen?* His footsteps thumped away—heavy and disapproving of her outburst. Evaan and Telia didn't like raised voices, it was a sign of uneasiness in the soul. As far as Kathy was concerned, it seemed to be the only way to get them to halfway listen.

The buzzing in her purse was a sweet distraction from the mess outside her door and she scurried to find her phone before it stopped ringing.

"Hello?"

"What's wrong?" Dave's voice demanded.

"My parents are here and I can't get them to leave."

"I'll be over in five."

"No, Dave. I don't want you to come." *Yes I do, desperately.* He'd be able to support her, tell her that she wasn't the one who was wrong. But her parents were so embarrassing and subjecting

Dave to that side of her life was something she couldn't let him see.

"Five minutes, Muffin." Then he hung up.

Relief washed over her. She would have backup. For the first time in her life there would be someone there for *her*.

Telia knocked on the door. "Kathy, honey. Where's your detergent?"

Of course they didn't bring their own. "Under the sink." With an engorged lump lodged in her throat, she opened the door and faced her parents.

"Like I was saying," her father announced, "we talked to Todd and he told us you were a little frantic and not yourself. It was hard for us to hear the news, too."

"Yeah," Kathy drew out. "I wouldn't say I was 'frantic.'"

"Oh, my dear." Telia came over and wrapped her arms around her daughter. "He is such a gentleman. Would always think of his lovers before—"

"Gross, Ma. Very gross." Kathy pulled away from Telia to lean against her empty counter with her arms crossed. "I can't believe you would give Todd my information. I am not okay with that."

Telia's large breath brought her bony chest up and straightened her back. "I thought you were over that teenage crush, Karma."

"Crush?" She opened her mouth to continue but the doorbell rang.

"I'll get it!" Evaan announced before Kathy could even move to greet her savior.

* * *

The door opened to a thin, grungy man with even grimier clothes. The smell that permeated from him made Dave take a step back.

This is Kathy's father? The realization would have been funny if he hadn't been so horrified. The stringy hair, the off-grayish color of his skin, and the yellow nails he was now chewing on made Dave's stomach sour.

"Is Kathy here?"

The man surveyed him while chewing. "Yeah." But he didn't move.

"Can I see her, please?"

"I'm her father and we're having a family—"

"Dave." Kathy appeared breathless and relieved.

"Hi, Muffin." He leaned around her father to kiss her cheek. "Thought I'd stop in before work and see if you wanted to ride in together."

"Oh, you work with Karma?" Telia asked. There was a slight slyness to her smile and Dave instantly knew that her mother didn't think he knew Kathy's former name.

"Actually I do work with Kathy." He smiled at Telia while reaching out a hand. "I'm Dave."

"Nice to meet ya, I'm Telia. My husband, Evaan."

The two men only nodded at each other.

"Do you want some coffee, Dave?" Kathy pulled him in by the arm.

"I would love some. So how long are you folks in town?" He caught Kathy's eye and winked, trying to ease her mind about her parents' arrival.

At first he thought of her as shy but now he truly saw the error of his thinking. The woman standing before him might be cautious but not the least bit unsure. No, this woman, Karma, was the one who fought to release herself from the restrictions of her family and was unmistakably determined to see them out the door as soon as she could.

"We're not sure." Evaan sat down at the tiny kitchen table.

"Dad, you should take a shower. You only have an hour before Dave and I leave for work."

"Well, why can't your mother and I stay here while you're out working for the Man?"

"I'll never understand why you'd want to work anyway." Her mother tsk-tsked her.

Dave saw and understood what these freeloaders were doing. "I like to work," he told them. "There's something fulfilling about it."

"I like being my own man," Evaan announced.

"I am my own man," Dave told him then took a casual sip of his coffee.

Evaan pulled himself out of the chair then just stood. His beady eyes narrowed on Dave. "That's what every man says when he wants to keep his job and impress his woman. I prefer the truth. Work sucks and I don't like doing it."

"Well, that may be..." Dave took his time sipping his coffee. "But I happen to actually enjoy my life—and job. It certainly beats the alternative. I really hated having to live off of others when I couldn't find work. It's kind of degrading, don't ya think?" He motioned with his cup for Evaan to agree but the older man turned and walked away.

"I agree," Telia said. "There's nothing like a job well done when you work for it. I'm gonna check on Dad and get in the shower too."

Kathy cleared her voice then glanced at Dave. "You want a bagel or something?"

"I'd love one. And a better kiss than the one you gave me when I came in."

"Well, if that's all." She wrapped her arms around his neck but instead of kissing him Kathy leaned her head on his chest. "This is terrible. Horrible."

"I'm glad I could be here with you."

"I didn't want you to meet them. They're awful people, Dave. My family isn't like yours."

His heart went out to her. She truly felt alone when it came to people being compassionate about her background—he understood the feeling well. "I'm sure they have their good points."

"Ha! Very few."

He stroked his hand over her hair while his mind wandered back to the carefree woman he spent the night with. The one he had been so close to telling the truth about wanting to spend the rest of his life with her. But he knew she wouldn't believe him, and now he understood why. Being raised by two people who thought only of themselves and found no shame in the fact they lived off their children and others was enough to make any person weary of love and relationships.

Chapter 14

The night crowd moved in as the early birds left. The weather warmed up to a balmy seventy-two. The smell of burgers on the grill had Kathy closing her eyes, relishing the fragrance and trying to forget the past few hours. How she yearned to have a place to cook like that. Be able to feel the sun on her back as she cooked her meal and talked to close friends and family. Charcoal was her favorite way to do it. The smoky flavor it transmitted to the food made her mouth water.

"Hey." Dave walked into her office, coffee in hand. "Here you go."

"Thanks. By the way, how's Louie working out at the bar? I was a little concerned with his age and being able to keep up." They hadn't said too much to each other on the ride in. It was just as well considering she'd been fuming about her parents' lack of movement to leave. But now that she was safe in her office, work soothed her to calmness.

"He's doing great. You okay?" He sat on the corner of her desk and sniffed the air. "I can't wait to throw some food on the grill tonight. Wanna join me?"

Her hands were dry, strange that she would notice that right now. She also needed to take her nail polish off. Working on one of the chipped nails Kathy finally answered him. "I'm good. Just—"

Dave bent his head to get a better look at her. When she turned to avoid his stare he got up and knelt in front of her chair. "Kathy?"

"Yeah?" She felt nothing. How could she explain that to him? When it came to her parents there were stages she went through. First, astonishment that they chose to be the people they were. Second, anger because she'd always disappoint them yet they felt they could rely on her. And lastly, nothing.

He placed his hands on either side of her chair. Not so much as to box her in but more for her to understand his seriousness about being there for her. Kathy recognized this but still crossed her arms and legs in defense.

"Please look at me."

When she did an overwhelming urge to weep came over her. "I don't like them, Dave. They ruin everything." A sob escaped her before she could prevent it. "I never wanted to be like them."

"You're not them, Muffin. Never were."

"I found them in bed with my ex-husband." The confession hadn't been her objective but now that it was out what could she do?

"What?"

"He was my dad's best friend and years older than me." Tears came to her eyes. She once promised herself she would never cry over Todd again, nevertheless here she was doing it. Maybe it was part of the healing process. Maybe this was what she had to go through to make her and Dave's relationship stronger.

"Sick bastard." The rage in his voice gave her comfort. No one in her childhood community had seen anything wrong with the affair.

"Todd said he was going to take me away from that way of life, that he loved me and would teach me how to be the perfect wife. Little did I know that meant he would beat me when I didn't do what he wanted."

Dave let out a long, slow, measured breath after Kathy's declaration. "How did your parents feel about this?"

She shifted in her seat. "Great. Wonderful. He was already a part of our family so why not? After I found the three of them in bed my mother tried to compare 'notes' with me." Kathy swallowed hard. "They've always had an open relationship when it came to sex."

Dave backed off a little, giving her room. "What did this guy say to you after you found them all together?"

"That he wanted to tell me but thought I'd react the way I did. And I also should be more understanding because I'm young and couldn't do for him what a more experienced woman could. Apparently I really sucked in the sex department." She looked back down at her hands and hoped Dave wouldn't see the painful turmoil inside her. The whole situation was as humiliating then as it was now. Why hadn't she been smarter? Known better? Weren't parents supposed to protect their children from stuff like this?

"First of all, you suck *really* well." Dave grinned when her eyes met his. "Second, this guy is a creep and deserves castration. He took advantage of a young girl. How old were you?"

"Sixteen. Eighteen when we were married and I found them all together." Somehow Dave's words made the statutory rape less shameful. Confessing to him seemed so much simpler than trying to cover the truth.

"You are a beautiful woman who overcame a hell of a lot. You're a survivor and deserve a man to treat you like a lady."

She uncrossed her legs and felt her stiff arms begin to relax. "Why? What is it about me that makes you interested? I'm defective. I never had an orgasm until I was with you. I failed a marriage to a man who found me completely boring in bed. I even fell asleep once during sex because I couldn't get aroused. What kind of woman does that?"

He looked at her with hard assessment. "Muffin, from the moment I first saw you I knew you were the one. I can't explain it and I don't know why. But I'm telling you, there is nothing wrong with you. That man should burn in hell. And maybe this is wrong to say but I hope your parents are right there with him. You were right to distance yourself from them, and now I get why you don't want them at your place especially when you're not there. As for your ex-husband, I think he's gay."

"What?" Her laugh turned into a snort. "Todd isn't gay."

"Really? Think about it. You're a smart girl. Whose best friend is he?"

"Sex just wasn't a big deal in our marriage. And he's a 'man's man,'" she quoted with her fingers.

"Ahh-aa."

Kathy marveled at the realization that Dave didn't have to force her to open up. It was so easy to be around him, to talk to him. "I'm a mess. You should run as fast as you can."

"Muffin, you don't know half the shit I've done. Screwing this up," he gestured a hand between them, "is my greatest fear."

"You might not feel that way after a few days with my parents here. And you haven't even met my brother yet."

"I'm not going anywhere so get used to it. You're where I want to be, Kathy. Why can't you understand that?"

Her voice became meek, even to her own ears. "Because no ever has."

"Stay with me again tonight. Don't go home." He leaned his forehead on hers. "I hate seeing you like this."

"I want to run, Dave. Just leave and never look back." To flee to anywhere but where her parents were.

Dave stood suddenly. "Would you leave? Get in your car and drive away?"

"No." The answer came to her without thought or question. "You're here and that makes me want to stay." Every "unrealistic" dream she ever had seemed to be tied to this one man. With him she felt she had it all, without him, there was nothing. No marriage, no children, or white picket fence to call her own. "I think I'm in love with you, Dave."

* * *

"Really?" While grabbing her hands to pull her to stand, his eyes grew wide with astonishment. "You fuckin' with me?"

"No...I...umm...I—"

He wrapped his arms around her waist and pulled her in for a red-hot kiss. Whatever thoughts played through his head, whatever retort to her non-acceptance of herself played second fiddle to the admission of her feelings for him. With her body molded to his and her confession of love still alive in the air he swayed them to the office couch, dipping her onto it. Lovingly Dave began his exploration of her lean body. Not being able to stop himself, he peeled away her clothes to observe the blush his touch created.

"You're so sensitive."

She pulled her jeans down and off one leg. "Take me, Dave."

"I love you." He was inside her so fast his body bucked at the quickness. First they were talking, then kissing, now... With his mind muddled and his body vibrating he pounded into her. Last night's escapade was a dim comparison. The desperate passion between them made their arms entwine tight around each other.

"Dave. Oh, my—"

The sound of his name coming off her sweet lips catapulted the need mounting inside him. "Hold on to me. Don't ever let go."

Everything in the world around them didn't matter anymore. The questions and second guesses evaporated into nothingness.

He wanted to weep. Never in his life did Dave feel so loved, so needed. The miracle of forgiveness that Kathy gave his spirit she could never possibly be able to understand. Though he lived the life of a reformed drug dealer, he never truly forgave himself for the hell he once put his parents through. But he knew absolution was given to one's self, not from someone else. And for the first time, here in Kathy's arms, Dave felt it and his spirit soared with it.

"You're everything to me," he whispered in her ear.

She embraced him harder. "Your confidence scares me."

She bowed under him while her lips trembled. His eyes seemed to roll back while his body became its own commander. Sensation after sensation painfully built until they both exploded in unison. Her inner walls tightened around him as his own expelled into her.

Panting and pink-faced, Kathy and Dave couldn't help smirking.

"Wow," she said.

"No kidding. We're not even naked."

"We're so naughty, Dave. This is my office."

"I know. Talk about a turn-on." He took her hands and cuffed them above her head. With that little action, he saw the passion start to grow again in her eyes. "You like me holding you down, don't you?"

"I could really get used to it." Flirtatiously she bit the side of her lip.

"What?" His voice demanded her to answer when he saw she wanted to say something else.

"I like the look in your eyes when you're doing it."

Bringing his mouth close to her ear, Dave whispered, "How about I tear your clothes off tonight?" Her walls clenched around him. "You make me unbearably hard. And now that you're mine, I'm going to fuck you every chance I get."

He slipped out of her and then inched back into that drenched opening. Her gasp is what pulled him back from taking her swift and hard. Slow. Mind bogglingly slow was what he wanted to do. This way she would feel every solid ridge of him and all the unexpected pleasuring aches. And while Dave's stamina had always been good, he found himself fighting the urge to finish quickly so they could make love again.

"Hey, Karma—"

Dave and Kathy both gasped at her parents standing in the doorway.

"Get out!" Kathy screamed.

"Why? It's not like your father and I haven't seen you naked before."

"Not since I was a child," Kathy shrieked.

Something close to a growl escaped Dave's lips. "Please leave so we can get decent."

Evaan huffed at the request. "Fine but I don't know what the big deal is."

Kathy covered her face with her forearm. "Oh, my God."

"It's okay, Muffin."

"No, it's not." She uncovered her face and looked him pointedly in the eye. "If they make any sort of move on you, tell me."

He laughed despite the seriousness on her face. "What?"

"They've seen you naked. That's all it takes."

"Really?" The absurdity of the situation suddenly didn't seem so funny. Her face drained to static white.

"Yes."

"I promise I will. And for the record." He tried to make the kiss as sweet and loving as he possibly could. She needed to know that she was the only woman for him. "I'm not even remotely attracted to either of your parents."

Chapter 15

Walking out of the office Dave's sole intention had been to kick both of Kathy's parents out of his restaurant. However he thought better of it. The most important thing his parents had taught him was that if people truly wanted to change, they had to do it. No amount of love and protection could do this for Kathy. She had to stand up to her parents on her own. But he would be by her side every step of the way.

"I really don't know why she's making such a big deal about it," Telia announced to everyone sitting at the bar.

"I'm with ya." Evaan turned to the couple—Dave's unsuspecting parents—sitting a few stools from them. "Don't you think after a certain age children shouldn't be embarrassed by their parents anymore?"

George looked at Evaan with curiosity. "I guess it depends on what you did."

"We embarrass our children all the time," Renee piped in.

"Yes, you both do," Jake commented with a frown.

"I just don't see the biggie," Evaan explained. "As if we all don't have sex. We've seen her naked."

"And," Telia added, "your son has a nice ass."

"Thank you?" Renee glanced at her husband then at a horrified-looking Kathy ten feet from them.

"I can't believe you said that, Mom."

"Why? The man is prime." She looked Dave up and down then licked her lips.

He felt like a piece of "prime" meat with creepy served on the side. Evaan seemed to have the same look when his gaze moved to Dave.

Kathy looked ready to blow. No longer was her face pasty white; now the deep shade of crimson showed her anger instead of mortification. Clenched tightly at her sides were hands white from lack of proper circulation while she stood rigid and straight as a pole.

Wanting to say something to cut the tension, Dave cleared his throat. "Ah-hum. How about a round of drinks, Jake?"

"Sure. Sex on the beach?"

Giving his brother a mild stare, Dave then moved to kiss his father and mother. "How you guys doin'?"

"Good." Renee took a sip of her martini. "Enjoying a different kind of conversation with Kathy's parents."

"I'm sure." Walking behind the bar, Dave began to help his brother.

"Little early for drinks," George commented to Renee.

"I need this," her voice grumbled before knocking the whole drink back. "Another, Jake."

Dave and Jake knew their mother well, and seeing that George didn't argue with her, he understood too. She was only trying to mellow out her temper. Renee had always been a fierce woman. Even as children they had feared her temper. As adults they looked to her for how to handle sticky situations like this one. She always seemed to be able to come out of a commotion with the least amount of scars.

"I think I'll have one too," Kathy told Dave.

"Aren't you working?" Evaan asked. "Or is what you were doing in the back room called 'working.'" He winked at her then turned to his wife. "I'd love to get hired here if that's all it takes."

"You're both gross. Give me a shot, Jake." Kathy swallowed it and then signaled for another.

"Telia." Renee turned to the woman with copper-colored hair. "You're quite a lady. What brings you both here? Besides Kathy of course."

"Well, we're pleading with our daughter to help us."

Kathy rolled her eyes. "Here we go."

Evaan spared his daughter a glance. "We really need phones. The ones we have aren't good and we can't get ahold of her if we don't upgrade."

Telia put her arm through Evaan's and leaned into him. "What if something happened to her and she can't get us."

"'Cause you'd be my first call." Kathy slammed the glass down and motioned for another. When Jake hesitated she gave him a look that would frighten the devil himself.

"She's so damn difficult. Never understood that family should share everything." Telia directed this toward her daughter.

"Not everything, *Mom*."

Dave cleared his throat again. "How long do you plan on staying?"

Evaan looked at his wife and then down at their joined hands. "Not sure. The vehicle needs repairs and its getting crowded with the three of us.

Kathy choked on her drink, literally. And as Dave ran around the bar to help, Renee stood up and started slapping her on the back. "You're okay, honey. I'm not gonna let anything happen to you."

"Thank you," Dave said to his mother. He then turned his

attention to the woman he loved. From the look on Kathy's face he had a pretty good idea who was with her parents—Todd. But he still hoped he was wrong.

"Our friend isn't well," Telia told them. "He's been traveling with us but really needs a bed to sleep in."

"There are some cheap hotels in the area," George suggested.

"We're more than a little strapped for cash right now." Telia looked at her daughter with mournful eyes.

"You both are so transparent it's sickening," Kathy told them with a little slur in her voice.

"Todd's sick, Karma. He needs a bed and—"

"He has your bed. You're not staying at my place. Forget it."

Evaan had the nerve to look shocked. "I can't believe you'd turn your own parents away."

Kathy gave a rueful laugh. "I'm a heartless bitch. Isn't that what you called me when I refused to pay for your cell phones the last time you made an appearance?"

Dave's heart went out to her. No child deserved to be treated this way by their parents.

"I was angry and with Todd being close to death we thought you'd be understanding. Obviously we were wrong," Evaan insisted.

"He's not knocking on death's door. I saw him a few weeks ago," Kathy said while waving her glass in the air.

"Yes, he is!" Telia rose from her seat and stood toe to toe with Kathy. "You loved him once and he still loves you. How can you do this? Your father and I—"

"Okay, everyone, out back." Jake motioned with his hands. "*Now*. I'm not in a business to have family squabbles in my restaurant."

"Oh," Stuart said, obviously disappointed. "It was just getting good."

"Sorry, old boy." Jake rocked back on his heels. "But if you want to follow them out back, I won't stop you."

Renee picked up her third drink, ready and willing. Dave considered telling her this was an argument between Kathy and her parents but knew it wouldn't do any good. When Evaan stood to head back, Jake cleared his throat.

"Ten-fifty. I'd rather you pay your tab before heading out."

Evaan looked at his wife, then Kathy, then Dave, and back to Jake. "But he said they were on the house."

"No. Dave gave one round to everyone. You had drinks before that."

Evaan puffed his chest out. "Are you charging them?" He thumbed toward George and Renee.

"My parents raised us and took care of us. We don't charge them, we charge customers."

"Oh my." Telia eyes began to water. "Are we going to have enough for everything we need?"

"Not our problem." Dave stepped forward. "You can't go into a restaurant, order whatever you want, and expect to get it for free. We'd be long out of business if that's how it worked."

Evaan threw down ten dollars. "She's poisoned all of you against us. We're not bad people."

"That's debatable." George took a long sip of his beer while keeping his eyes on Evaan and Telia.

"Ten-fifty," Jake repeated, while motioning to the lonely bill.

"Telia, honey, let's get out of here. It's obvious these people aren't going to help us." He dug in his pocket and threw down all the change he had but still held short on his tab.

"Shame on you!" Telia seethed. "Not helping others who have less than you. Total snobs."

"We help those who help themselves," Dave told them. "And

by the sound of it, you prey on the kind-hearted. Good thing we're not. Right, Dad?"

"You bet."

"Karma, we'll speak about this later at home." Telia raised her chin and spun toward the door.

"No, we won't. I don't want you in my apartment, I want you to leave."

Evaan and Telia walked out of the Lion impervious to what their daughter said.

"Damn it. This was just getting good." Everyone turned and looked at Stuart who shrugged his bony shoulders. "You get to be my age and this is where you go for action."

"Another shot, Jake," Kathy announced by slamming her glass down onto the counter.

Every muscle in Dave's body tensed and his jaw ached from grinding his teeth. *Lowlifes* repeated continuously through his mind. Swallowing hard, he moved to Kathy's side. If this was how he felt, he couldn't imagine how she did.

Kathy downed her drink just as her cell rang. Flipping it open, with more force than necessary, she told the caller, "Not now." And hung up.

"Who was that?" he asked.

"Nobody."

But it had been somebody and Dave really wanted to know who. He followed her back into the office where they had made love only a half hour earlier.

"Who was that?"

Kathy swept her arm across her desk and sent papers, pens, pencils, and whatever else was on it flying. "Nobody."

But his distrusting mind couldn't let it go. She didn't treat people like this and he didn't like how she was reacting. "I want to know who it was. I can make it right."

"Excuse me?" She turned on him as tears streamed down her face. "What does it matter? You can't fix everything, Dave."

"You won't know that unless you give me a chance. Who was it, *Kathy*?" He didn't mean to growl out her name, it just happened. And with that bite of anger in his voice, Dave realized he better get himself under control before he pushed her away.

"Go bully someone else. I'm sick of being the scapegoat and punching bag. I deserve better than that. And you know what? I'm gonna have it."

"I'm not bullying you. I just want to know so I can help."

"Too bad!"

Disbelief over her lack of trust forced Dave's voice to rise. "I deserve to know, Kathy!"

"Why? Because we slept together?"

"Yeah. No. You're my woman and—"

"Go to hell. I'm my own woman."

"Was it your ex-husband?" When she ignored him, his heart crumbled. "I've tried to earn your trust. I have done everything I know how to and yet you still won't let me in."

"And this is why," Kathy's meek voice pointed out as she backed away from him.

"Don't do that. Don't back away from me because we can make this right—together."

"No, we can't because this is how it's always been and how it'll always be," she said while crossing her arms.

"It doesn't have to be, Kathy." With his patience evaporating quickly, Dave tried one more time to reason with her. "You can start changing this whole mess right now by telling me who that was on the phone."

"No."

"This is bullshit, Kathy." Dave slapped a hand down on her desk and leaned toward her. "You want love, trust, and respect? Well what about me? Don't I deserve it, too? What are you hiding?"

"I'm not hiding anything," she told him.

"Then why can't you even look me in the eye?"

"I don't want to talk about this anymore." When she attempted to walk past him, Dave moved in her way.

"You know, Kathy, you don't want to be like your parents and yet in some ways you really are. Look at your place. Empty. As if you're afraid to put down roots. Here I am trying to be there for you, and you're pushing me away."

Wide-eyed and shaken Dave braced for the slap that never came when she stood before him but said nothing. "Well?" he asked.

Kathy merely moved around him and out the office door.

"Really?" he called after her. "You're going to run like they do too? Not think twice about who you're leaving behind?"

"What's going on?" George asked.

"Nothing."

"Something," Renee insisted.

A black cloud of sadness shrouded him. "She walked out on me without a word."

Renee took her son's face in her hands. "She needs time."

"I've given her time, patience, and love." He looked around his empty office. "She's not coming back."

"You don't know that," George tried to convince his son.

"Doesn't matter. It was only a matter of time anyway."

Renee placed her hands on her ample hips. "Now that's just stupid talk."

"Maybe but it's true. You guys were right; I shouldn't have said anything about my past."

"First of all," George began, "we never said you shouldn't tell her and—"

"Nope, you didn't come out and say it but I should have known better. Hell," Dave laughed at the reality that was just starting to sink in, "she was probably looking for a way out and this was the perfect opportunity."

"What's going on?" Jake asked.

Dave turned to Jake. "I fucked this up, big time, and Kathy left. I doubt she'll be back."

"What! We need her, you jerk." Jake patted his brother on the back, none too lightly. "It'll be okay. She's a chick, bro, they're all emotional."

"Maybe." He sat with his head in his hands. The beginning of a bad headache was knocking on his temples. "I feel like I'm going to be sick."

"Yeah, well…you can't. We have a business to run and there's three more hours of your shift left."

"You're going to make me work it?"

"What the hell gives you the right to be surprised? Kathy just walked out and we're already two short tonight and starting to get busy. Dad said he'll help behind the bar and Mom will take orders. Your pussy ass is going out there, Kathy or no Kathy. You started something and by God you're going to finish it."

"Geez, Jake. You don't have to be that way about it." Dave stood with the weight of three tons on his shoulders. "I wasn't gonna give you a hard time."

"Good."

Chapter 16

The tears didn't stop coming for days. Kathy tried to reassure herself with ice cream and chocolate but it didn't help. Then she tried meditating and fasting for hours on end, which only succeeded in giving her slim frame a more waif-like appearance. Sophie attempted to talk her into calling Dave or at least going to work; however Kathy just didn't have it in her. She wanted to crawl into a hole and die. The betrayal she felt over Dave's words hadn't so much as shaken her as it disappointed her. He obviously didn't know her.

Looking around her vacant apartment, Kathy sighed heavily. When she had gotten home that day her parents and Todd were waiting for her. They started by apologizing for making a scene at her job. Then they assured her that they weren't mad at Dave or his family for the way they had treated them. The moment her father spread his arms wide to welcome his only daughter into them, Kathy lost all control. She slapped her father across the face, looked at Todd with such venom that he backed away from her, and then announced to her mother that she was the worst parent to have ever been given the gift of children.

This time there would be no mistaking her words or actions. She wanted them out of her life forever. When their vehicle was still parked in front of her building the next day, she called maintenance to have it removed. The whole situation felt surreal.

When her parents pleaded with her to let them stay, she informed them, "I have already helped you enough. If you don't want me to call the police and have you removed along with your van, I suggest you find a new place to squat."

Todd had the audacity to look shocked. "I'm dying," he pleaded with her.

"Go to a hospital. You've caused me pain for the last time."

With the memory still reeling in her mind Kathy ran to the bathroom sick to her stomach. The pain of letting Dave go paled the problems with her folks. He had called her every morning. Showed up and waited hours outside her door. Sent countless flowers and even apology cards for what he said, written and signed with love. Yet her mind wouldn't forgive him. How could she? He was wrong, she was nothing like them.

With an aching heart she relived that day up to the moment when her parents came walking in. The dream had been there and real. *Every couple gets into fights,* she told herself. *Then they make up and move on with their lives together. What's stopping me?*

Her cell chimed with Sophie's ring.

"Hi."

"Hey, Kathy. How ya doing?"

Another person who called every day to check on her. "I only threw up once today. So I guess that's an improvement."

"Yeah, it is."

The silence seemed to last a lifetime. In the decades they'd known each other, never had they not found something to talk about. However Sophie's boyfriend was Dave's brother and that one fact seemed to constantly come into play.

"Dave's miserable too."

"I know, Sophie."

"Kathy, I think you two should talk. Neither of you are going to move forward if you don't."

"I know." The misery in her voice left an acidic taste in her mouth.

"It's been two weeks. I can't keep filling in for you at work. I'm starting to feel taken advantage of."

"I know, Sophie." Wow, was she pathetic or what?

Sophie huffed into the phone. "You know what? I've been nice long enough. You want to throw away the best thing to ever happen to you? Fine. I'm not going to watch you destroy yourself over a little argument. Thank God the two of you didn't get any more serious because turning and running at your first argument is pretty darn pathetic. And I told Dave the same thing! Obviously you're not ready for a relationship with a decent man. No. You want to spend your time depressed over your past mistakes and not doing anything to correct them for the future. You suck, Kathy!"

"I know, Sophie. You're right. I'll call him today. I'm looking for another job."

"What? You have to be kidding me!"

The disbelief in Sophie's voice made Kathy smile. "No, I'm not."

"I am right, though."

"Yes, you are, Sophie. I need to get myself together. But everyone needs to be patient. Heck, I lost my boyfriend and my parents in one day. I have a right to mourn."

Her friend stayed quiet for a moment. "I wish it all hadn't happened that way."

"It's for the best. I can't carry them any longer." Her scoff into the phone seemed callous but well deserved. "I just can't figure out why they would come here. Maybe their drug use has gotten worse."

"Oh, I'm so sorry, Kathy. You shouldn't have had to go through all that."

"No reason to be sorry. It seems the only person that hasn't hurt me lately is you."

"Remember what happened with Jake and his flashback? When I went to his home and he didn't know I was there?"

"Yeah."

"Remember how he never wanted me to see him again and how he couldn't understand how I could forgive him for hurting me?"

"This is different, Soph."

"Not really. At the time you were upset that I stayed with him."

"He could have really hurt you."

"But he didn't. I knew right then that I was willing to go through all the bullshit to have him. Jake is the one for me."

"What are you saying? I should be able to put up with Dave's crap?"

"No. I'm saying he's willing to put up with yours."

Kathy's disapproval of Dave's words stopped at the tip of her tongue. "Excuse me?"

"I told you, I'm not going to sugarcoat this anymore. I'd hoped you'd come to your senses by now but obviously I was wrong. You're no prize, Kathy Mae Smith. You have trust and abandonment issues, conflict issues, and are in need of a man who worships the ground you walk on. Dave is that man. I saw it the first time you two met. You can't deny it, you love him."

"You think I'm messed up? What kind of friend tells you that? Who the hell do you think you are? I'm not the one who's screwed up here. He is."

"He's not the one running and refusing to let you in. He's the one who's been trying to make it up to you because he loves you. He's the one who's still going in to work every day despite all this. Do you know your parents came in to see him after you made them leave?"

"What? The gall of them trying one last-ditch effort to get money."

"Yeah. And he threw them out when your mother said she was there to get your paycheck for you. He told them they should be ashamed of their actions and that it's too bad they'll never know what a beautiful woman their daughter is, inside and out. That man loves you unconditionally. I'm not saying what he said was right but damn, Kathy, give him another chance."

Kathy sat on her bed shocked at the revelation. "I'm the messed up one, aren't I?"

"I wouldn't love you if you weren't."

"I guess I just figured it was Dave." It all came together in one nice little package. In Sophie's relationship it was Jake who needed the extra care. In her relationship with Dave she was the one who needed the extra push. "Why didn't you tell me sooner?"

"I thought you knew." A small chuckle escaped Sophie. "Do you know the difference between psychotic and neurotic?"

"No. But I have a feeling you're going to tell me and I'm going to feel better about all this."

"Psychotic is when you don't know you're crazy. Neurotic is when you do. Now that you know which one you are, the healing can begin!"

Kathy closed her eyes and had a good laugh. "I need to shower. I'll call Dave afterward."

"You sure?"

"Yeah, I want this so badly. It makes me sick to be without him. I don't know if I can make it work though."

"Now's not the time to doubt yourself. You've overcome so much already."

"You're right. And I *will* talk to him. Promise."

"Good. And anytime you need a butt kicking, just let me know. Heck, I'll do it even if you don't need it!"

* * *

"Damn, I'm looking scruffy." Dave rubbed the long stubble on his face. In the last week he began to see where he went wrong with Kathy. In the last few days he understood he shouldn't have said she was like her parents. God he missed her. Countless times he picked up the phone to call for their morning chats and then remembered he messed things up and needed to be apologizing. He let her down when he pushed too hard. Hadn't she asked him to be patient and to trust her? Dave wanted what Jake had with Sophie. Unconditional love. But instead of trying she left; like he always knew she would.

He sprayed the foam in his hands and rubbed it all over his cheeks and jaw. With a few swipes of the razor, he began to look more like himself. The last glide drew blood and he swore ripe when the phone rang at the same time.

"Hello," he snarled.

"Dave."

His heart leaped in his chest as hope sprang to life inside him.

"Kathy, please don't hang up," rushed out of his mouth. "I'm so sorry. Please—"

"Dave, you don't have to take the blame for everything. I had a part in it also," she said.

"Yes, but I said some terrible things and I didn't mean to. I... and... I miss you so much. Please come back to me."

"I needed space, Dave."

"I know. I tried. Well, in the past week I've tried." Five days to be exact. He hadn't sent flowers, cards, phone calls, nothing. He gave in to the fact she didn't want him in her life.

"I'm sorry. I made a mess of things." When he attempted to interject, Kathy cut him off. "Don't even say I didn't. There was no reason for me not to tell you it was Sophie on the phone."

"Why can't you trust me, Kathy? I've never done anything to make you to think I wouldn't understand."

"Maybe that's it. You're too understanding, too perfect, and it scares me."

"Do you want this to work?"

"I..." She took a deep breath and the agony of the wait elevated his anxiety. "I love you, Dave, and that's all that counts. I don't care about my parents and what kind of marriage they have. I don't want to be scared of us because we might fail. Dave, I'm not perfect. I need a lot of maintenance and sometimes I might get scared and attempt to run. But just promise you'll help me. Work through this with me. Can you do that?"

His mind spun with what she'd told him. "Ummm, can we go back to the beginning? To the part where you said you loved me. Because I want to know exactly what that means to you."

Razor forgotten, Dave grabbed a towel for his face then headed to answer the pounding at his door. There, with her hair a mess and dark shadows under her eyes, stood Kathy.

"It means I won't accept anything less than all of it. I want a picket fence, a dog, kids, and you by my side every night. If I go a little crazy from time to time, I want you to pull me back and show me how much you care. I didn't grow up with the kind of life I want to have with you. But I think your parents will help show me how to be good at it."

"They'll show us."

"I love you." A tear rolled down her cheek and he wiped it away with his thumb.

"I've loved you all my life. Even when I didn't know it was you."

"Damn it, Dave! How the hell am I supposed to react when you say stuff like that?" She walked away from him and back again while his laughter filled the doorway. "I don't think this is funny."

"I think it's great!"

"Why?"

Dave grabbed her hand and pulled her into his home. "Because I love you and we don't have a clue what we're supposed to be doing."

"I didn't want you to be in love with me. Still don't. I don't understand what I'm feeling. I look at you and I think to myself, 'you're gonna break his heart. Run.' Then I wonder what it is that makes me want to be with you, near you." On a huff she placed her hands on her hips. "What makes you think you're in love with me? Because I know I'm not easy to handle sometimes."

"Let's see." He tilted his head in examination of her. "You talk soft but have a mean streak."

"Is that supposed to make me swoon?"

"Ha! No." He stroked her cheek with his thumb. "You have a wicked sense of humor. Your eyes mesmerize me like I've been put under a spell. You put me in my place when it's needed. You're truthful, loving, and a little unsure." Leaning in, Dave's smiling lips kissed hers gently when he saw the flash of insolence in her eyes. "Damn, you turn me on with those defiant looks, Kathy." He lifted her into his arms. "I'm going to strip you down and keep you that way for the next twenty-four hours. Then we're going to have dinner with my parents and let them know we're getting married. Can you handle that?"

"I love it when you tell me what to do." She wiggled her brows at him.

"Oh, then you're going to love what I have in mind right now." He headed back to his bedroom. "You have a lot of making up to do for the crap you did."

"Oh, no. Please don't make me be your sex slave."

"Too late." He grinned. "You need to be taught a lesson."

She bit his earlobe and lust shot straight to his groin. "What if I'm naughty again?"

"Then I tie you up and have my way with you." Her small gasp delighted him. "Thought you'd like that."

Chapter 17

Dave rounded the city block corner whistling. No, he never thought his life would turn out this way. But here he was ready to take the next step with the woman he loved. Asking Kathy to marry him hadn't been a hard decision. She understood that he had certain quirks and respected them, just as he did hers.

The week seemed to pass quickly. The two of them made plans to work on the outside of his home again. And when his mother tried to give her input on what plants and flowers to put in, Dave only smiled. Maybe she was right about the bushes being a pain to take care of but she wasn't going to talk him out of getting the yard fenced in. Someday they wanted kids, even talked about it after a sweaty romp in the hallway. Then he'd taught her how to flip burgers on the grill. They laughed so hard when the patty flew into the air and landed on the grass.

Perfect. That's what his life was.

A crease of worry formed on his brow. Why couldn't she come to dinner tonight? She just said there were some things she needed to take care of and to trust her and she'd explain everything later. It was too bad because his parents were looking forward to seeing her before they went back to Florida and he wanted to tell them the good news together. Kathy's lease would be up in two months, she would be moving in with him, and they would be starting wedding plans. He imagined his parents being ecstatic. Could see his mother crying and his father cheering. Dave figured a ring for Christmas, wedding in summer, honeymoon wherever her heart desired, and a child the following year. Of course with Jake and Sophie's news, his parents probably would have had a couple heart attacks from being overjoyed. An uncle. He was going to be an uncle. Jake looked scared, Sophie seemed tired but happy. They'd wanted to wait until Kathy was there too but Sophie couldn't stay quiet any longer. They had found out only an hour prior and hunted Dave and his parents down to tell them.

With his feet barely hitting the ground, Dave skipped across the street to the parking lot to his new pickup truck. It was just one more thing that made his life wonderful. He had his woman, his parents, his brother, his health, and a brand new black Ford F-250.

The night had become warm and with it the night life heated up. Women with low-cut shirts and short skirts flaunted their legs with high heels. Men whistled as they walked by and flexed their muscles while smoking cigarettes. Did he miss that? *Naw.* He couldn't see the purpose of it anymore; not with Kathy in his life and a future ahead of them.

About to unlock his door, Dave spotted her familiar silhouette. Walking with careful steps, Dave made his way over. Four car lengths from the couple he stopped and stared. His mind rejected the image before him while his body refused to move any closer. There she stood, Kathy, the love of his life. The woman he had been waiting for and couldn't wait to marry standing there embracing someone else.

A dark cloud of hate shrouded his thoughts. She'd been too busy to meet him and his family for dinner because something came up. Yet here she was locked in another man's arms while they talked closely. When the mysterious man tried to kiss her, Kathy moved her face away and exposed her neck. *She likes that spot being kissed.*

Taking a half a step toward them, Dave stopped. He knew he should confront her, confront them, but he couldn't bring himself to take another step. *She's your woman, go and get her.*

But as he willed his legs to move in their direction, the man's lips captured hers. By the streetlight Dave could see Kathy's hands fisted in his shirt. Unable to torture himself anymore, he turned and walked away. He'd gotten about ten steps when he heard her voice.

"Oh, God! No! Dave!"

"Too late!" He yelled over his shoulder and jumped into his truck.

"Dave, wait!"

He could hear her calling his name as she ran toward him but he paid no mind and pulled out of the lot. In his rearview mirror he saw Kathy and her lover standing side by side. The man put an arm around her shoulder and Dave's stomach twisted from disbelief.

"What the hell were you thinking? Stupid!" He punched his dashboard, the pain never registering from the hit to his fist. "Idiot!"

Jesus, even his parents loved her. They were going to be devastated. The weight on his shoulders was substantial.

Instead of heading home, Dave drove to the seedier side of the city. The place he used to call home and one, he figured, would always welcome him back.

"Fuck it!" He pulled into the back of the strip club and parked in the darkest spot he could find. No use advertising his presence. Outside of the bar stood a man smoking. The nostalgic smell of cigarettes and marijuana filled his lungs. Yeah, he was home.

* * *

"No! And get your damn hands off of me, Todd!" Kathy fell against the stop sign pole. How did this happen? She just lost her dream man for the second time. How? Violent tears streaked down her face. Her heart wasn't only broken but destroyed.

"Sweetheart. Come on." Todd put a reassuring arm around her shoulders and tried to bring Kathy to her feet.

"You asshole!" Her fist connected to his groin and Todd went down. "I hate you! I hate you! Why did you come here?"

"I wanted to make it right," he grunted out.

"I told you I'm with someone. I love him!" Saying it aloud startled her. At first she had doubted the love, then questioned if she was capable of being in it, now she knew she would give anything for it.

"You loved me too, once." Todd coughed. "Damn it, Karma."

"I never loved you like I do Dave!" Kathy swiped at the black mascara smearing across her face then ran to her car.

"What the hell? You're going to leave me here?" Todd yelled. "He'll never love you like I do! He'll leave you and you'll be back because I'm willing to forgive your limitations."

Zipping out of the parking lot she saw a cruiser with flashing lights come roaring toward the scene. *Good.*

Kathy pulled out her cell and dialed the only person she was certain would know where Dave could have possibly gone.

"Sophie, this is an emergency. No, I haven't gotten into an accident but I think…actually it wasn't me it was my idiot ex who really screwed things up. I'm looking for Dave. This is a mess. Please call me back!" Kathy drove straight through the red light and passed the strip club.

* * *

"Hey, Dave, haven't seen you here in a while."

"How's it hanging, José?" Dave took a seat at the bar. "I'll have a shot of the strongest thing you got."

"Comin' right up."

José poured the dark liquor and Dave downed it. When he pointed for another, the bartender obliged. "So how's the family, José?"

"Divorced," Jose told him with his heavy Spanish accent.

"Told you not to marry a stripper, didn't I?"

"I believe you did. But damn the things that chick could do."

"Kids?"

"Naw. You?"

"Nope." Dave stared down at his empty glass. "Thought I might someday."

"Me too."

José moved down to the other end of the bar after he filled Dave up. The numbing effect of the auburn liquor soon spread throughout his body. *Good, don't want to think anyway.*

"I couldn't believe my eyes. Now I think I'm dreamin'. Sanders, what the hell brought you back to me?" Charlie sniffed hard and rubbed his nose. It didn't take a seasoned coke addict to know what the man had been doing in the back room.

"I needed to drink and a place to hide."

"Well out here isn't gonna do it." Charlie gestured for Dave to go with him. "Come on."

"You know, Charlie, I think I'm gonna stay out here," Dave said. "Hey, José! Set me up again."

The bartender smiled. "I can do that."

"Sanders, when an old friend invites you to their private party, it ain't nice to turn 'em down."

Dave glanced at the heavy hand on his shoulder. "You're right. I'm not partying, though. I'm drinking." *What are you doing here, Sanders? Look at this guy, he's drunk, high, and you should get your butt out of here.* Dave turned on his bar stool to face the stage. "And watching a show. Got some nice-looking girls."

"Could get you a private dance in the back."

"Thanks, Charlie, but I'm really not looking for that kinda fun."

"Suit yourself. You know what to do." Charlie nodded and walked to one of the bouncers. Dave saw the mountain of a man look at him and then back at his boss. *Yup, I'm being watched. This was such a mistake.*

Turning to catch José again, Dave asked for a beer.

"You know that's gonna make you sicker than a dog tomorrow," José advised.

"Yeah, but I deserve it," Dave announced.

"I'm surprised to see you here."

"I needed something familiar." Dave watched the woman on the pole, while trying to clear his mind.

José spoke something in Spanish and turned away from him.

"What?" Dave asked.

"Nothing"

"Speak your mind, José," he slurred as he contemplated leaving to find a quieter place to sulk. "You never were shy about it before."

After filling an order the old friend leaned on the bar toward

Dave. "You're loco. Get out of here," he told Dave in a hushed tone. "You got out with your life and now you're back? Stupid, *amigo*. You're real stupid."

Dave studied the scene around him. He once thought of this place as his home—somewhere to do whatever he wanted to. Now he understood it was a lifestyle that pulls you down deep into the abyss of darkness and then chains you there. What was he doing there? Instead he should have been making things right with Kathy. He could have misunderstood the whole scene he saw. Right? Dave scoffed. He deeply wanted the whole thing to be a mix-up but he saw what he saw.

Against his better judgment Dave planted his empty beer on the bar. "Get me another, José."

* * *

"For God's sake, Dave, pick up the damn phone!" Kathy was pulled over in front of Jake and Sophie's place trying to think of anywhere else Dave would be. She had already been by the Lion, his house, called Mitch, and her own apartment.

Dragging her feet and with slumping shoulders, Kathy confronted the front door with guilt, disgust, and hope. If anyone would know where Dave went, Jake would. Before she could raise her hand to knock, the door swung open and Jake stood there, hands on his hips and a scowl on his face.

"Hi, Jake."

"What the hell is going on? You look terrible."

"Nice to see you too," Kathy mumbled.

Jake moved out of the way and swept a hand to signal her to come inside. "Have you heard from him? I've called and called but he's not picking up. What the heck happened?"

"No, I haven't heard from him and was hoping you'd think of a place he'd go."

Jake shook his head "no." "Honestly, Kathy, the guy doesn't do much so you'd think he'd be easier to track down. What happened now?"

Kathy opened her mouth to confess the sin but Sophie came into the room groggy and a little off balance. "Have you found him?" she asked.

"No," Kathy told her.

"You want some coffee or something?" Sophie yawned and then moved toward the kitchen. "I'm making myself some tea."

"I'll take coffee," Jake announced.

"Okay, but you're putting your own cream in it," Sophie joked.

Kathy's heart yearned for an understanding like that. To know each other so well that even the smallest of jokes made you smile and love the other person more. She wanted that with Dave.

"It's not my fault you can't get it right." Jake kissed her on the top of the head. He then turned to Kathy. "What happened?" he growled.

"Umm," Kathy cleared her throat. "Well, it's this whole crazy thing with my ex."

Sophie dropped a tea bag in her water. "Todd?"

"Yeah. You see Dave kinda saw him kissing me." Kathy bit the side of her lip and closed her eyes tight. She didn't want to see the disappointment in their eyes due to her betrayal.

"What!" Jake yelled. "What? Dave loves you. How the hell can you betray him like that?"

"There's more to it, Jake. You have to believe me. I never meant for any of this to happen."

"Then how did it happen?" he commanded.

Instantly flushed and ready to weep Kathy opened her mouth

but only a squeak came out. She already missed Dave so much. The way he'd smile at her from across the room. How he'd take her hand at random moments and squeeze. Then there was the love she felt every time he held her—she was going to miss that the most.

"Kathy." Sophie took her hand. "You need to calm down and tell us what happened.

"Calm down? How the hell am I supposed to do that? I run into my ex who makes a mess of my relationship with the man I love then he kissed me. I tried to push him away and couldn't, Dave saw us then sped off. I kicked Todd's ass, and now Dave is missing. Get worked up? I'm already there!" Kathy insides were trying to rip their way out of her body from the silence Jake and Sophie were giving her. "Well?"

"We can't find him, either." Jake walked away from her to stand next to Sophie.

"Oh, no." Crushed, Kathy braced herself on the counter next to her.

"Kathy, can you think of anywhere he'd go?"

"I've tried everywhere I can think of." Kathy eyed Jake's back. Somehow this was all her fault, no matter how unintentional her actions may have been. "I'm sorry Jake."

"Yeah, well, you can make it up to me by finding my brother." He stomped across the kitchen and poured himself a coffee.

The home became eerily quiet. Kathy's thoughts and fears tormented her as she grasped at every ounce of hope but only found disgrace and blame. She started to weep again for all she didn't get to say to Dave and all they might not be able to share in the future. Every part of her body shook as she struggled to find any kind of solace in her new reality—life without Dave.

Jake turned on her. "Stop crying!"

"I'm sorry!" Kathy held onto her head hoping the rotation would stop before she fainted. The tiny white lights flashed under her eyelids to let her know she was close but she refused to give into the darkness. Dave needed her, she needed him, and that was first priority.

"Jake—" Sophie darted to her friend.

"No, Sophie, I've had enough of her blubbering. My brother is out there hurting and I want to know where!"

"I don't know, Jake! I don't know where he'd go!" Kathy screamed. "I didn't do anything!"

"You were kissing another man!"

"No, I wasn't! He kissed me and I pushed him away. I did nothing for Todd to think I'd take him back!" She wiped her face with a damp facecloth Sophie had fetched from the bathroom.

"Jake—"

"I swear to God, Kathy, if my brother is in some kind of trouble because of you I'll—"

Kathy became hysterical. There would be no consoling her now. She couldn't understand the words she attempted to say to Jake but in her mind the apology and worry must have gotten through because he closed his eyes, and Kathy saw a tear slide down his face.

"I can't lose him, Kathy."

"Both of you stop it!" Sophie yelled. "We're never going to get anywhere if all we do is yell! Jake, let's go back to Dave's house. Your parents are probably worried. And I need to lie down."

"Why?" Kathy's world revolved again but this time she was able to stabilize it by concentrating on Sophie's face. "Are you still sick?"

"No. It's wicked late and I'm pregnant. We announced it at dinner tonight."

Kathy smiled as a genuine feeling of warmth and love bloomed inside of her while she wiped her tear-streaked face with her arm. "I'm so happy for you two." She stood and hugged Sophie then turned to Jake. "Are you excited?"

Jake stern jaw twitched. "Yeah, sure! I'm already picking out baby names. We're going to call him Buck Wild Sanders. Or Trixie if it's a girl."

To mess with Jake Kathy said, "Soph, don't twins run in your family?"

"Awww, I think I'm gonna be sick," Jake said while turning a light shade of green.

"Must be a stomach bug going around," Sophie suggested. "I was sick all morning."

"I'm so sorry, Jake. I was only kidding." Kathy moved past her girlfriend to comfort the expectant father.

"Jesus. I can stare down the enemy. Shoot and hit a target hundreds of feet away but the thought of being a father terrorizes me," Jake told both women.

Kathy rubbed the big guy's back. "You're going to be a great dad, Jake.

Sophie raised her hands in defeat. "We aren't going to find him like this. Kathy, where have you checked?"

"I think we should drive to the Lion," Jake suggested. "And where's my damn coffee?" He clomped around the kitchen in search of it.

Defeated Kathy followed him, "I've already been there."

"We might have to check his old stomping grounds," Sophie told them. The emptiness in her voice confirmed it was the last thing she wanted to say, do, or think about. "Just to be sure."

"He wouldn't go back there," Jake insisted. "He just wouldn't."

"Sophie's right. We should think about checking." Kathy's stomach churned as her voice hitched. "This is all my fault!"

Sophie frowned into her tea. "He's an adult and makes his own decisions. When we find him we may not like what he's done but we'll need to be understanding."

"I'm telling you," Jake insisted with a slam of his coffee cup. "He won't go back to those places."

Before another word could be spoken Kathy's cell phone rang. In desperation she dumped her purse on the kitchen table and sifted through the pile to find it.

"Yes? Hello? Dave?"

"Actually, Miss Smith, I was looking to see if you've seen Mr. Sanders," Detective Owen informed her.

"What? Why are you looking for him? What's going on?"

"Miss Smith, please calm down."

"Calm down! People need to stop telling me that! Dave's missing and we can't find him anywhere. You just happen to call looking for him and—"

"There was some trouble at a downtown strip club and Mr. Sanders's truck is here."

"Where?" Kathy wanted to know.

"What the hell is going on," Jake demanded.

Kathy put a finger up signaling for him to give her a moment while Detective Owen continued to explain and give her an address. Her mind rushed in every direction as the fear of not knowing told her to panic. "We'll be there as soon as we can."

"Well?" Sophie asked.

"There's a strip club downtown called the Triple X—"

"I know the one," Jake grumbled.

"Apparently Dave's truck is there but he's not. The place got robbed about a half hour ago and a bartender was shot." But what happened to Dave? Why was his truck still there?

"Let's go!" Jake jumped to attention and grabbed his jacket.

"Kathy, we'll take your car. I have a spare key to Dave's so I'll get it out of there before somethin' happens to it."

Sophie weaved a little as she stood. "Let's go."

"You should stay here," Kathy told her and Jake agreed. "You don't look so good."

"I'm fine, damn it, and I'm going!"

Kathy's brows scrunched together at her friend's outburst. "I'm sorry Sophie."

"Don't be. I'm a little testy, that's all." She shrugged her jacket on and looked at Kathy. "Sorry."

Twenty minutes later Dave was still nowhere to be found. If he had been in the bar no one was talking. Charlie, the owner of the place, only smirked at Jake and said he hadn't seen him. It was obvious the man was lying.

"I don't understand," Kathy said to Jake. "Why wouldn't he tell us the truth?"

"Because men like that don't know what the truth is, Kathy. They lie so much that their views of the world are warped," Jake explained.

Sophie looked around with a helpless frown. "Now what?"

"Don't know," Kathy told her.

"Kathy? What happened? And I want the whole story." Jake asked as if reading her mind.

"Oh, this big crazy mess, Jake."

"And?" Sophie put an arm around her friend.

"And I might have really screwed things up by not telling him the truth right away."

Jake looked at the sky and let out a long, loud puff of air. "Lying is never a good thing."

"I didn't lie. I just didn't tell him." Her defense sounded pathetic even to her own ears. And now she might have lost the one person who loved her completely for who she was and where she'd come from—the one person who would protect her from her family. "I'm such an idiot!" No longer able to stop herself, Kathy fell to her knees in the Triple X's parking lot. "I can't believe this is happening. We have to find him. What if he's dead?" she demanded while glancing at Jake.

The large man only fidgeted on his feet. "Don't do that, Kathy. Come on, stop crying, get up."

Sophie bent down and wrapped an arm around Kathy. "He's not dead, Kathy. And, Jake," she said while turning a stern look his way, "be more supportive."

"I am!" he insisted. "Let's go to the Lion and see if he's there so I can choke him for making all of us worry."

Sophie rolled her eyes at Kathy. "Sorry, this is Jake being helpful."

Chapter 18

Thank goodness he had strong hands to hold up his head because without them Dave feared his noggin would otherwise roll off. He'd been sipping on coffee for the past half hour after downing a few pills. His stomach wasn't feeling that hot either—as if it had been lined with hot lead that was slowly melting into his intestines. Yeah, he was going to be real sick but first he wanted to make sure he was good and sober for it; this way he could yell at himself for being such a dumb schmuck. Dave shook his head. He could have gotten himself into some serious trouble by going to the Triple X, and then where would he be? Not only would he not have Kathy but he'd have let his family and himself down. Dave had worked too hard for too long to flush it all away.

When Dave's body lunged forward in a massive heave, he ran to the bathroom to purge the night's mistakes away. As he rested his head on the seat of the bowl he found a little humor in the situation. It had been a long time since he had drunk himself sick and now he remembered why he swore to never do it again.

Rising from the porcelain throne, Dave headed to his office for the toothbrush and paste he always kept in there.

Toothbrush in mouth and brushing vigorously, Dave stepped out into the bar area and came to a halt. There stood his brother holding Dave's coffee cup, Sophie telling him to calm down, Kathy who was staring at him with tears streaming down her face.

"Oh my God," she whispered. "You're okay."

Jake and Sophie turned toward him—shock, surprise, relief on their faces. Running to him, Jake picked Dave up in a bear hug, and spoke, "You son of a bitch! Do you know how worried you had Sophie? She's been beside herself, and Kathy…" He put his brother down and glared at him. "The girl won't stop crying and I can't take much more of this. I don't know what the hell happened but you two need to make this right," Jake demanded.

"I was only looking for a little time for myself. I really don't see why everyone's so freaked out." Dave defended himself. "Geez."

"Don't know why?"

Sophie put a hand on her man's arm. "Jake, relax."

"Relax? I'm going to kick his ass. First he runs off and doesn't answer his phone. Then he leaves his truck at the Triple X without an explanation—"

"My phone died and I didn't have a charger with me. I had been drinking at the X but didn't want to drive." Dave shrugged. "So I took a cab here for some quiet." No, he didn't want to look at Kathy. She'd been kissing another man after she had promised to spend her life with him. Yet looking at her now, seeing the dark lines of worry streaked across her face, his heart told him there truly was more to the story than what he saw.

"Dave." Kathy stepped to him. "You're okay?"

"Yeah, I'm fine. Well, except my heart." It might have been a crappy thing to say but Dave couldn't help telling her the truth. He only felt half a man without her.

As they stared at each other, Jake cleared his throat. "I'm going to call Mom and Dad—"

"Really, guys?" Dave's shoulders dropped. "This wasn't that big of a deal."

"Well, it felt that way." Sophie tapped Dave's cheek with her hand. "And if you ever do this again. I'll be the one to kick your butt."

"I don't know why everyone is so mad at me. I'm not the one who was kissing someone else." The words blurted out before he could stop them and he instantly regretted them.

"That's not what happened."

Dave shot a bland look her way. "Then you've got a lot of explaining to do."

"Tell me about it," Jake griped.

"Well I'm first." Dave nodded his head toward the back office.

Kathy's agreement was quiet. "Okay."

He followed Kathy's shuffling feet to the back room. "Could you hurry up, please? I'd like to get this over with." He heard her give a slight whimper and checked his temper at the office door. There was no need to make her suffer when her own conscious was doing it for him.

"Dave, you have to believe me I never meant for anything like this to happen."

"I hope not because this is a pretty messed-up situation. I thought you wanted to spend the rest of your life with me."

"I do. I just…well, you see there's this whole thing with Todd—"

"Obviously." Standing before her was excruciating. Every inch of him wanted to take her in his arms. He didn't know he could love someone so deep that forgiving this type of betrayal was bittersweet; being able to hold and love her but never trust her.

"You don't understand. Detective Owen wasn't coming around to look for you, Dave, he was watching me."

"What?" Never in a million years would he have come up with the idea that it was her the cops were after. She didn't have a criminal past and she sure wasn't hiding anything he knew about.

"My parents showing up and the stream of robberies isn't a coincidence. Detective Owen figured it was only a matter of time until they came to find me."

"But why? And that still doesn't explain why you were kissing your ex. Your parents have nothing to do with this." Dave crossed his arms in defiance.

Kathy sat on the office couch and buried her head in her hands. "Dave, Detective Owen asked if I'd help him trap Todd. He's wanted in multiple states. He's a pedophile."

"Excuse me?"

"That's not the worst of it." She looked at him then, sad and defeated. With no choice of his own, Dave went and sat next to her.

"Tell me," he said while putting an arm around her shoulders and pulling her in close to where he wanted her to be for the rest of his life—in his arms.

"Todd also is the primary suspect in my aunt's murder. I didn't know she passed away a few weeks ago and left me her entire estate."

Silence. What words could he find to comfort this latest blow from her parents? They deceived her on so many different levels. And yet she had seen through them right from the start and had never given in to their words of love and guilt. Shame on her parents for not caring about what they'd done to their only daughter by defending a wanted pedophile.

"What happened with Todd tonight?" Dave finally asked.

"I was going to meet up with everyone after I had a meeting with Detective Owen. He asked if I'd be willing to set my parents and Todd up." She took a deep breath. "Despite everything they've done to me, it was still hard, Dave. They are my parents; not very good ones but they're the only ones I've got."

"I'm so sorry, Kathy." Dave wrapped her in his arms and kissed the top of her head. "What you did tonight was very brave."

"It wasn't supposed to happen like that. I didn't know Todd had followed me there. And when he grabbed me and tried kissing me I thought, 'This isn't happening. Where is Owen to get this freak away from me?' Then I saw you." She looked up and into his eyes. Dave saw not only her fears and worries but the burning question: "Did I ruin everything between us tonight?"

The question was a sock to the gut. All the air in his lungs rushed out of him, leaving a dizzy feeling in its place. She wanted to know if she ruined everything between them? Hell, it wasn't her who almost did that, it was him by running away and not demanding an answer right away. "Forgive me, Kathy."

"What? You didn't do anything wrong."

"I didn't fight for you when I should have. I should have walked over to that jerk and laid him out on the pavement."

"It's okay. I did that after you sped off." There was a little glint in her eyes showing how proud she was of how she'd handled her ex.

"That's my girl." Unable to put off the yearning any longer, Dave cupped her chin in his hand and kissed her. "I love you so much."

"Oh God, Dave. I love you too. I thought I lost you and—"

He broke her train of thought with another kiss. Words

weren't needed to heal what happened because there was nothing to forgive.

Kathy's body melted into his as the kiss went deeper. Everything he was, everything he'd been working for, all led up to this moment. And now that he had her, Dave was never going to let go. "Let's run away and get married."

"What?" Kathy blinked at him.

Dave cupped Kathy's face in his hands. "This weekend, let's take off to Vegas and get married."

"I…um. What about your parents and Jake and Sophie. And—"

"Thank goodness you're okay." Renee came bursting into the office. "We were worried to death!"

"Honey Bunny, can't you see they're making up?" George asked his wife.

"Yes, yes. But I needed to see that my boy was okay."

"I'm fine, Mom." Dave got off the couch and went to hug his mother. "It was all a misunderstanding."

"Thank God," George stated. "Because we really like her."

Dave smirked. His parents were the most awesome people he knew. How could he not love them?

Renee smiled at Kathy. "Why don't you two come out? Detective Owen will be coming by."

"Can you just give us one more minute?" Kathy asked.

"Sure, honey."

Dave's parent's left while muttering at each other.

"I told you they were making up and not to go in there," George told his bride.

"And I told you I didn't care," Renee replied.

Kathy turned to Dave with a smile. "They're the best."

"Sure are."

He was so cute standing there with his hair a mess, his shirt-tail only half tucked in, and the look of love in his eyes. "I can't believe you'd even consider not inviting them to our Vegas wedding. They would totally make it fun."

Dave pressed his lips together in an attempt to not smile. "You don't think I can make Vegas fun?"

With her hands on her hips, Kathy cocked her head. "Hmm. I don't know, what else did you have planned besides nuptials?"

"How about a class hotel with a large bed and room service?"

"So." Kathy walked to Dave and looped her arms around his neck. "You only want to keep me in bed the whole time."

Dave snickered. "Well, yeah! The thought of becoming an uncle really has me thinking about children and I was thinking we should get a lot of practice in before we try for real."

Nibbling on his ear, Kathy asked, "I like how you think, Mr. Sanders. But what about sightseeing and the casino?"

"Whatever you want," he told her on a winded breath. "And don't you think being married to me is gamble enough?"

Kathy threw her head back in laughter. "We're such messed-up people. I'm so glad we found each other. Don't ever let me go, Dave. Promise me."

"I promise to love you and never let you go, Kathy." With a hand to the small of her back, Dave pulled her close. "Let's sneak out the back door."

"Let's get out front so everyone doesn't think we have."

Kissing her on the nose Dave said, "See! I need you to make sure I don't do things I should do. Or is it that you having me thinking about doing things I shouldn't be?" He gave her a considering look.

"HA. Speak for yourself. You're the one who just talked me into a Vegas wedding."

She kissed him and poured every part of her soul into it. This man was going to love her forever and it was a healthy, real, and solid relationship. Kids, a house, and maybe a dog; she couldn't wait.

"Hey!" The banging at the door broke their kiss but not their bond. "You guys coming out here or what?" Jake asked.

Chapter 19

Thank you for coming, detective." George moved in front of his oldest to shake the detective's hand.

"I have to say, when Mrs. Sanders called and asked for me, I was a bit shocked. Miss Smith, how you holding up?"

Everyone's eyes peeled to her. Not sure what to say, Kathy turned it back to him. "Detective Owen and I had a meeting yesterday. I'm so glad you're here. You can clear things up better than I can." She glanced at Dave with an open heart.

"I've been investigating a couple who'd been involved in a large sting, south a bit, many months back but we never were able to catch the responsible parties."

"Kathy's parents," Dave said with disdain.

"All we knew is that it was an older couple and we suspected they had many others working with them."

Dave's eyes met Kathy's, and with that connection she saw his love and understanding for all that had happened in the last few hours. Oh how she wanted to leave all the ache and turmoil in the past where it belonged. When Dave wrapped his arms around her, Kathy realized the nightmare truly was finally over.

Owen cleared his throat. "Last night I was following up on a credible lead."

"You mean, following me," Kathy filled in.

"Right. This couple was supposedly traveling with a known pedophile and—"

Kathy closed her eyes and swallowed hard. *Known pedophile.* There was so much in those two words; they meant her parents knew what Todd did and approved; it meant they were okay with him doing it to her; and it meant there were more victims out there.

"—selling drugs. They are also suspects in many of the robberies that have been happening around here and a murder."

Kathy stared down at her feet because she couldn't think of any other place to look. *Murder.* One simple word that meant so much when paired with someone you love.

* * *

Dave held her tighter and wanted to tell her it all would be okay. But how could he?

"It's okay," she whispered to him.

"No, it's not," he told her.

Detective Owen turned a frown on Kathy. "We have reason to believe that Todd Doyle is the perpetrator who entered Miss Smith's aunt's home and killed her."

The gasps in the room would have been audible to the deaf.

This poor woman was all Dave could think. He was just happy she was in his arms now. He held on a little tighter, hoping she'd understand how much his heart was bleeding for her.

"That monster got what he deserved and it felt really nice to kick his ass," she told him.

"She sure did, Mr. Sanders."

"That's my girl," Dave chuckled.

Kathy bit her lip and furrowed her brows. "I was trying to find you and explain what happened with my aunt. I'm sorry it got so out of hand."

"There's nothing to forgive, Kathy. You and me, we're all right. And getting married in Vegas," he whispered in her ear.

From behind him, Dave heard his brother ask, "So, detective, you arrest this guy?"

"Yes. And the couple he was traveling with." Compassion displayed clearly on Owen's face. "Miss Smith's parents were taken into custody early this morning after we got a clear ID from the gunshot victim."

"Oh you poor girl!" Swooping in Renee pulled Kathy into her ample arms. "How dreadful."

"It's okay, Renee. This has been coming for a long time. Now they can't hurt anyone else."

"After you left the Triple X," Owen explained to Dave, "it was robbed and a bartender was shot."

"What?" Dave's mind whirled. "Who was hurt?"

Detective Owen pulled out his notebook. "Stan Waitt."

Relief flooded over him. José was all right.

"I wasn't looking at you, Mr. Sanders," Owen told him. "I was watching Miss Smith to see if her parents would show. And with your past, well…." He let the rest of his sentence hang in the air.

"I understand."

Owen looked around the bar. "Well, I'm done. Miss Smith, I'll be in contact. Sanders…" All three men gave a "yeah." "I'll need you to come in and give a statement about what time you came into the Triple X, what you saw, and when you left."

"No problem." Dave watched him leave and with the detective's absence a clear, heavy apprehension filled the space.

"Guess he wasn't as big of a jackass as we thought." Jake wrapped an arm around Sophie's shoulders. "Come on, let's get you home."

"Yes." Sophie looked dead on her fatigued feet. "This sucks." She gave Kathy a hug. "You okay."

"Yeah, I'm fine." Kathy wrapped her arms around Dave's waist.

"Okay, I think we need to let these two talk," Renee announced. "And when you're done I want to know the wedding plans."

"For goodness sakes, Honey Bunny."

"I want a wedding damn it! I'm finally getting a grandchild, I deserve a wedding."

Dave and Kathy stared at each with twin smirks.

"What?" Renee and Sophie asked.

"What does everyone think of Vegas?" Dave asked.

Wide-eyed Jake looked at his brother. "You got to be kidding me."

"Nope, dead serious."

Kathy clapped her hands together and bounced. "Can we get hitched by Elvis?"

Dave once again cupped her face in his hands. "Whatever you want."

"One month," she told him. "I want a dress and everyone there."

Renee jumped up and down while clapping. "It's a wedding! A wedding, George!"

George pulled his wife to him. "I know," he told her with a loud kiss.

"Ah-hm." Jake cleared his throat. "You know, Sophie and I

have been talking about tying the knot—with the baby coming maybe we—"

"Yes!" Kathy and Sophie announced.

"We should get remarried too!" Renee told her husband.

"I think that would be wonderful." Kathy held a hand out to Dave's mom. In that moment he knew she'd never have to worry about her parents again. Now she'd have the ones she deserved. Ones that would appreciate her, love her as he did, and never give up on her.

Dave looked at her just as Kathy choked on the tears she'd been trying to hold back. The need to fall to his knees in front of her was strong and forceful and appeared imminent. She had needed him last night and had been coming to tell everyone what was going on. For the first time she would be opening up and trusting him and his family to be supportive—and was asking for help. That must have been hard for her. To find out her parents were going to be arrested, to be part of that plan.

"I love you," he told her.

"I love you, too."

A few minutes later Dave was locking the front door to the Lion after his family left. "I think that went well," he told her.

"I think this is going to be one heck of a wedding."

"I agree." He walked to her with other things on his mind. "I'm going to make up for not being there for you last night," he told her.

"You don't have to do that, Dave. It was all a misunderstanding."

"No, I think I really need to." He wiggled his eyebrows at her.

"Well, if you insist," she told him, catching on to what he was hinting at. "I think it's an excellent idea."

Epilogue

I don't know, Jake, they look like they might be burning."

Jake picked up his son, threw him into the air, then caught him. "What do you think, Ian? You think auntie's burning our lunch?" The little boy giggled as Jake continued to toss him.

"Watch," Dave told his brother with an elbow nudge. The two men were witnesses to Kathy attempting to roll a hot dog on their new grill. First she tried picking it up with the tongs, then she tried rolling it, which only succeeded in sending the frank off the grill and into the grass for the dog to eat.

"Damn it," Kathy scowled.

Dave cupped his hands around his mouth and yelled, "Nice try, honey."

She turned to him and waved the tongs with menace. "I don't care how many years it takes, I'm going to get this grilling thing down."

"In the meantime, the twins really need to eat." Sophie picked up her daughter who had waddled over. "Right, Tabitha?"

The little girl shook her head up and down. "Yes!" she shouted.

"Not fair, Sophie. That's all she can say." Kathy went back to rolling her hot dogs and then attempted to flip a burger. "Why do they always have to stick to the grill?"

"Watch this," Dave told his brother with a wink. "Honey, why don't you let me take over?" Dave walked to her and placed a hand on Kathy's large, rounded tummy. "You're having a hard time reaching is all."

"Are you saying I'm fat? You better not be saying I'm fat, David Arthur Sanders." Kathy pressed her lips together to keep from grinning.

"I'm saying it might be too hot for the little guy." He took the grilling utensil away from her.

"No, you're not. You're making fun of me."

"Never," he said with a smile. "I love you too much for that."

THE END

Please see the next page for a preview of

Seducing Mr. Right.

Chapter 1

The first step and the hardest step are often one and the same.
Sophie repeated this pep talk while her insides shook and her
stomach turned ripe with bile. She was ready for this change and
had been working toward it despite everyone's objections and
her own apprehension. After all, Greenwich, Connecticut, was a
long way from the outskirts of Boston, and many of the socialites
in her parent's circle believed only a lower class of people worked
in bars.

"This is the bar. Obviously." Sophie's new boss, Dave, turned
and grinned at her. "We open at two and close at one-thirty
Thursday, Friday, and Saturday. Two to ten every other night. We
serve small meals, typical bar food stuff."

Sophie listened as the man before her went down the list
of what her manager job would entail at the Hungry Lion
Bar-n-Grill. Excitement bubbled inside her as nerves danced
beneath her skin. Deep in thought about what she could bring
to her new position, she ran her hand along the silky wheat-
colored bar counter. The sun streamed in through the stained-
glass window, which portrayed a fierce lion battling a man with

a sharpened stick. The walls were a light tan and the stool covers and booth seats bloodred. Her heels clicked on the scarred, wood-paneled floors as she walked to the back.

"And this is the office." Dave opened a door and nodded for her to enter.

At first, nothing seemed unusual. The walls were mostly bare and a drab blue. Under the only tiny window in the room sat her desk with multiple piles of papers laying in wait. Everything was clean and—Sophie stopped abruptly at the sound of snoring to her left.

"Lord's sake!" Dave yelled. He turned and gave an apologetic smile to Sophie. "My baby brother, Jake." Dave lifted a booted foot and pushed on the sleeping man's bare back. "Jake! Where the hell are your clothes?"

Feeling a little flushed, Sophie examined the slumbering man. Jake was covered only by his boxers, and his muscular back and legs were left bare for her hum of approval. A harsh scar—*that must have been a nasty wound*—stretched down his left side, while a cleaner, surgical one ran just below it. When he shifted and threw an arm over his head, Sophie took an appreciative glance at the tree-trunk arms peppered with pockmarks.

"Jake."

Jake made an inaudible noise and burrowed deeper into the cushions.

"Don't disturb him on my account. We can work around him."

"Well, I don't think we'll be able to move him, anyway. Damn kid. Must have been celebratin' pretty hard last night to stay here. He's got a key to let himself in since he's been helpin' with the books. As much as I'd like to tell you this doesn't happen, it does from time to time. I was just hopin' you wouldn't find out until you were here for a while. This doesn't change your mind about the job, does it?"

Sophie looked at the mostly nude man sleeping on her office couch. If she wanted this job, then she was going to have to get used to the ways of the bar-n-grill scene. "Oh, I don't know, Dave. Coming into work every now and then and finding a naked man on my couch doesn't seem like such a hardship."

Dave laughed and gave Jake another hardy push with his foot. "At least you have a sense of humor about this. Okay, let me get the computer booted up and I'll show you what we've screwed up."

"You're screwing up my sleep, right now," the strained voice from the couch announced.

"Where the hell are your clothes, Jake?"

"I don't know, but I'm cold."

After much effort to suppress it, Sophie let out a good-natured snort. "Sorry," she told Dave.

"Not your fault." Dave grabbed a threadbare blanket from the office closet and covered Jake's massive body. "You'd never know we were brothers. This man works out like it's his job."

Sophie really tried to look disapprovingly at Jake but knew she didn't quite pull it off. The few men of her past never had physiques like that, and they each tended to have more of a feminine build.

"And that. That sparkle in your eye," Dave said, while pointing a finger at her, "is why he does it."

She glanced down at the sleeping man, now covered up by an afghan. She desperately wanted to uncover him but didn't dare. So instead, Sophie relived the memory of his strong naked torso and legs. She would definitely have a little fantasy about him later. After all, Sophie was a woman who appreciated a good-looking man.

Two long hours later, after sorting through old paperwork and files on an even older computer, Sophie realized they were in a bigger mess than Dave had let on. Maybe this job was exactly where she was supposed to be. Promotional ideas popped into her head for how to create more income and spend less—problems the Hungry Lion seemed to be having.

She eyed the sleeping figure across from her. They could always host a woman's night with male dancers. A sly smile crept across her face. Maybe Jake could make up this terrible first impression by hosting it...or dancing in it. Who knew, maybe it was one of his side jobs. *With a body like that, he must be doing something that requires plenty of strength.*

As if on cue, Jake rolled over and off the couch. He landed with a loud thud and grunt. Sophie sprinted out of her dilapidated office chair and to his side.

"Are you okay?"

Jake looked at her with red-rimmed eyes. She could see him trying to focus on her face and not quite getting the control he needed. "Who are you?"

"The new manager. Are you all right?"

"Yeah." Jake brought his knees up to his chest and rested his head on them.

Feeling the need to soothe the giant, Sophie petted Jake's curling brown hair. It was shoulder length and in bad need of a cut. "Jake," she whispered.

"I think I'm going to be sick."

Sophie snatched her wastebasket. "Here."

"Jesus. Where are my clothes?" At her chuckle he turned to her. "This is not funny."

"Oh, it absolutely is. Your clothes are on the side table."

"How did I..." His eyes rolled a little, and Sophie put an arm around the massive man to keep him from falling over.

"This is what I want you to do. I went out and got you some Gatorade and you need to drink it. You're probably dehydrated, and that's making you even sicker than whatever it is you drank."

"Maybe I don't want to."

"Maybe you don't have a choice."

"Okay."

He sounded pathetic and Sophie couldn't help chuckling. She grabbed the bottle and gave it to him with the cap off. The container looked unbelievably small in his hands, and a flash of what it would be like to have them on her caused a heated blush to rise to her cheeks.

"Let's get you back on the couch." He moaned when she put his arm over her shoulder. "Now, you need to help me Jake, you're a big boy and I'm a small girl." *Who would love to be under you, over you, wherever it is you'd like me to be positioned.* She gave a small giggle at her perverse thoughts. If Jake was one of the perks to working at the Lion, she was really going to enjoy her new job.

* * *

Jake woke a few hours later. The bugles in his head were finally silenced, and the drums had ceased to play. But Jake felt as if they had been replaced by the vice now squeezing his skull. At least he'd slept, even if it hadn't been a fully restful slumber. He didn't wake up soaked in sweat from fighting imaginary demons trying to kill him.

He rolled to a sitting position and sniffed. The cook seemed to be making something greasy. The delicious smell of cooking oil filled his senses, and Jake briefly wondered if his new recipe was being tried out. At least his stomach didn't turn and lurch at the aroma. He would take that as a good sign.

Bit by bit, Jake scanned the old storage room that became

their office. Something was different, and he couldn't quite put his finger on it. But then again, he wasn't really in the right frame of mind to be concentrating on anything. His brain began to clear, and the distant memory of a lady's voice broke through the fog. She had helped him drink the power drink and given him a damp cloth on the back of his neck when he heaved in what he assumed was the wastebasket next to him. The embarrassment of someone taking care of him caused nausea, once again, to threaten the reversal of his already empty stomach. Jake was a military man—he took care of people, not the other way around. With one hand holding his head and the other reaching for his pants, Jake heard the door open.

"Good. You're up."

He couldn't see who owned the sweet voice, but he knew it belonged to the woman who'd nursed him earlier. Slowly, he turned his head to look at her but she was out of his line of sight. Resigned to the fact that he was only in boxers and didn't remember how he had been stripped down, Jake tried to pull on his pants.

"Oh, dear. Here, let me help you."

Jake looked into his rescuer's soft blue eyes and small freckled nose. The primal male in him wanted to see the rest of her, but the miserable head on his shoulders wouldn't allow it. She smiled and helped him to put one foot in his jeans and then the next. With a little aid, Jake stood and she pulled them up.

"I think you can take it from here."

"You're not going to zip them for me?"

She scoffed at him. "And miss you struggling? No."

He watched her walk around the steel desk and sit. "That's my desk." At her questioning brow, Jake elaborated, "I keep the books for my brother."

"So I have you to thank for this mess?"

"Mess? No, they were like that when I got them. Where are my paper piles?"

"Organized." She smirked.

He brought a hand to his head then sat back down. "Shit. What the hell happened last night?"

"That's the million-dollar question in the bar right now. Apparently you came back here with Trixie."

"Trixie? Do I know a Trixie?"

"Well if you didn't, you do now."

"I'm sorry. Who are you?" At the knock on the door Jake moaned and the woman in front of him got up to answer it.

"Thanks, Dave. No, you can't come in."

Jake heard his brother grunt, "I don't see why not."

"Because you can harass him once he's off my couch. But right now I want him in a good mood in case he plans to camp out in here any longer."

"I'm not camping out," Jake grumbled. "And who the hell are you?" He watched her bump the door shut with her hip as she balanced a bowl of soup in one hand and a sandwich on a plate in the other. There was something graceful and precise about the way she did it.

"I'm the new manager. Dave told me to tell you, 'You know, the one I told you about yesterday before I left.'"

Jake cringed. "I'm such an idiot. Sorry. If my head would just roll off I could get out of your hair."

"Here, eat this. It's chicken broth. Forget the sandwich."

Taking the bowl from her, Jake looked at the woman before him. She had light brown hair, very tiny hands, and red glossed lips. He licked his own in response to staring at them. He supposed she must have seen him doing it, because she shifted on her feet and moved back behind the desk.

"Eat," she urged him.

"Thank you... Umm, I still don't know your name."

"Sophia."

"Just Sophia?" It amused him to see her roll those large doll-like eyes.

"Sophia Agnés. They call me Sophie. And, you are?"

"Jake Sanders."

"Jake?"

"Yeah?"

"Eat your broth or it's going to get cold."

He saw it. The quick flick of the eye when it shifts to see something clearer and then moves back just as fast. Her gaze had gone to his chest. Uneasy, Jake tried to remember the last time a woman had looked at him bare-chested. Sophie sat with her hands folded in front of her watching him, clearly trying not to notice he was still half-undressed and scarred. Suddenly it felt like that dream where he was giving an oral report in high school, only to look down and notice the only thing he had on was his underwear. A strange feeling, seeing that up until a little while ago, that *was* all he had on.

Jake put the soup down on top of a small filing cabinet then gave her a weak smile. "I'm chilly." He bent and picked up his shirt then slid it over his head. "Thanks for mothering me. Not much of a first day, eh?"

"You're forgiven. Now at the risk of sounding rude... I need to get back to reviewing your revenue. Or lack thereof." The look on her face told Jake of the hopelessness she felt toward balancing the books, then she started clicking keys again.

"If you need any help, just give a holler. Actually, please whisper today." He discovered he liked making her smile. It brightened up her face and showed in her eyes. Jake hoisted himself off the couch and picked up his bowl of soup. As much as he would have liked to stay and make her flash that grin again, he knew he should get out of the way so Sophie could work. Besides, he probably smelled as bad as he felt.

"I wouldn't go out there, if I were you." He turned and saw she never looked up from her computer. "Stay. At least you'll have peace and quiet. They're planning on razzing the living hell out of you, and I don't think you can take it yet."

"Why do you think that?"

"Because you're still green."

He laughed because she was right. He felt a little green and besides…looking at a lovely lady sitting behind a desk wasn't such a hardship. "Would it bother you if I went back to sleep?"

"Only if you don't eat the soup first."

* * *

The day went by quicker than Sophie thought possible. She made a mental note to bring in some small plants and pictures the next day to make her new office cozier. When Jake finally left for home to sleep off the remainder of his hangover, there'd been hoots and hollers from the patrons. Sophie felt kinda bad for the big guy. He'd only wanted to get out without being harassed, and he'd even contemplated trying to squeeze through the office window. Sophie had assured him there was no way he would fit.

Once home, she slipped on her pink fuzzy slippers and ran down the day's activities to her childhood friend, Kathy. The one person she could always count on and would always listen to.

"Sooooo, how's the new job?"

"Good." Sophie took a bite of her lasagna while cradling the phone to her ear. "Dave, my boss, is pretty cute."

"Really? Tell me more."

"He's tall, dark, and handsome."

Kathy made a gagging noise. "Really? You can't come up with anything better than that?"

"Okay, okay. He's much more your type than mine. Dave is supernice, very considerate, and has nice lips. His brother has a great body," she added under her breath.

"What? What! Speak louder, girl."

"Dave's brother, Jake, was passed out on my office couch for most of the day, and half-naked. Kathy, I don't think I've ever seen a man with a body like his before. I mean he turned me on just by lying there."

Kathy giggled into the phone. "Yum. What do you plan on doing with this hunky brother?"

"Nothing. I wouldn't know what to do with a man like that, and I'm terrible at flirting."

"Oh, come on! Have a little fun. Plus, your parents aren't here to reprimand you, so go wild."

"He looks like trouble."

"Even better."

Sophie gave out a loud huff. "I'll tell you what. If I change my mind and decide to start a little something with a man who can make you sweat with just a glance at his arms, you'll be the first to know and my mother the last."

"Promise?"

Sophie let the cloak of doubt guide her next words: "I don't know, Kathy. Maybe it's too soon."

"Hmmm…maybe you're chickenshit."

"Could be that, too."

About the Author

Once Rebecca Rose picked up her first romance novel she knew her destiny was typed on those pages. She lives to find romance in ordinary life doing everyday things, and believes we only need to be mindful enough to find it. While being slightly dyslexic creates some challenges, she feels compelled to write about the characters who reside in her head.

Now with multiple books published, she is a full-time writer with a nag for a muse who even talks obsessively in the car. That is, of course, when the voice can get a word in edgewise with her three children and husband of nineteen years along for the adventure.

Rebecca hopes her writing brings you to laugh, cry, and rejoice with her characters. Maybe even leave a lasting impression on your soul.

CPSIA information can be obtained at www.ICGtesting.com
Printed in the USA
LVOW12s1453150215

427121LV00001B/47/P